LUIGI FERRO
THE RHYTHM OF DEATH

Luigi Ferro
The Rhythm of Death
Story by Matt Borne
Copyright © 2024
Cover by Mats Ingelborn
Images by A.Karnaushenko, Kiuikson,
Master1305 & Wirestock
ISBN print: 978-91-89822-66-5
ISBN e-book: 978-91-89822-67-2
Published by Yabot AB, Sweden, 2024

1

The sun dipped low in the sky, casting a golden glow on the ancient stone walls of San Marino. In the heart of this storied city, the music festival pulsated with life, the rhythm reverberating through every cobblestone and narrow alleyway. At Piazza della Libertà, a sea of bodies swayed to the beat, their hands raised to the heavens as if to catch the fleeting notes that soared above them. The air was thick with the scent of heady perfume of youthful energy and unbridled passion.

Yet, even amidst all this chaos, there existed a man who tried to find solace from it all – Luigi Ferro, weary private investigator by day, lost soul by night. It was on this particular evening that I found myself perched in my office, desperately trying to shut out the cacophony of the festival raging just below me at the Piazza. My small sanctuary, adorned with dusty tomes and fading photographs, offered little respite from the relentless beat that seemed to penetrate my very being.

Leaning back against my worn leather chair, I closed my eyes and attempted to escape the noise, if only for a moment. Instead, I found myself drawn towards the window, like a moth to a flame, and pulled back the curtain to witness the spectacle unfolding before me. The festival grounds were a kaleidoscope of colors, with decorations draped across the grand stage built by the Palazzo Pubblico, and a sea of animated music enthusiasts swaying to the hypnotic beats.

The facade of the old town hall was clad in an enormous banner in black and orange, advertising the energy drink Energia Eterna. Obviously the main sponsor for the festival along with our local radio and TV station SMTV.

The pulsating music did not give me the silence I craved to chase away the ghost of a case I couldn't forget. A lost child, a pond, a discovery that arrived too late; the images haunted me, persistent and unyielding. The festival, a stark contrast to the quiet despair that filled my mind. Music, pulsating and relentless, invaded my chambre, a reminder of the world moving forward while I remained anchored to a moment in time. The beats, meant to celebrate life, felt like an affront, each note a taunt against the silence I craved.

I tried to shut it out, the joy, the laughter, the life that carried on despite my stagnation. Yet, the music demanded attention, a call to the living that I couldn't ignore. It was madness, this conflict between the desire for quiet to mourn and the relentless beat of the world's drum, urging me to move, to feel, to live again.

Closing my eyes, I sought refuge in darkness, an attempt to mute the relentless music that seeped through the walls. Yet, in the void behind my lids, the girl's face emerged, as vivid as when I'd found her. If one could just close one's ears as easily as their eyes, perhaps the music, with its false promise of joy and escape, could be silenced. Perhaps then, the echoes of her laughter, the memory of her smile, wouldn't find me in this self-imposed darkness.

But sound, unlike sight, isn't so easily dismissed. The festival's rhythms invaded my sanctuary, a relentless tide against my resolve. Each beat, a reminder of a heartbeat stilled too soon, of a life snuffed out before its melody could fully unfold. In the silence of my mind, the cacophony outside grew louder, the beats merging with the rapid pulse of loss, of guilt, of what-ifs that lingered like specters.

With every note that filtered through the cracks of my resolve, her image grew clearer, a specter in the silence I had crafted as a shield. The music, meant to heal, to unite, now only deepened the chasm of my grief, a relentless reminder that some echoes, once set into motion, find no peace, no silence, but linger on, indelible and haunting.

The case had taken something from me, a piece I feared I wouldn't reclaim. The child, innocent and gone too soon, left a mark, a reminder of the fragility of life and the weight of responsibility I bore in my line of work. The pond, once just a body of water, now held a reflection of my failure, a mirror to the doubt and the questions that lingered long after the case had closed.

The festival, with its cacophony of sounds and sights, seemed a universe apart from the quiet grief that had settled over me. Yet, it was there, in the midst of that chaos, that a shift began. The music, insistent, wove its way through my defenses, a reminder that life, in all its complexity, marched forward. It was madness, yes, but also a lifeline, a pulse in the stillness that had become my existence.

I stood, drawn to the window, compelled to witness the celebration that I had tried so fervently to ignore. Below, the piazza teemed with energy, a vivid tableau of movement and color against the backdrop of the city. The music, now a lifeforce, connected the crowd, a shared heartbeat that pulsed through the square.

In that moment, the divide between my grief and the world's joy narrowed. The music, once an intruder, now spoke of resilience, of the capacity to find harmony in the aftermath of discord. It was a call to healing, to finding the rhythm in the chaos, the melody in the silence.

As much as I desired to escape the darkness that lingered in my mind after my last case, there was something about the raw energy of the festival that piqued my curiosity. Perhaps a part of me yearned to be amongst the crowd, to lose myself in the throes of desire and temptation that seemed to radiate off their bodies like heat from a flame.

As midnight drew closer, the anticipation in the air was palpable, a seductive undercurrent that wove its way through the pulsing throng of bodies below my window. Aurelia La Duca, or DJ Ecciti as she was better known, the siren of the night, was poised to take center stage, and her devotees waited with bated breath, their desires laid bare in their feverish eyes and impatient gestures. I could not deny that she possessed a certain magnetism, her fame and talent eclipsing those of the other performers like the resplendent sun drowning out the stars.

From my vantage point, I observed as the stagehands made their final preparations, their movements precise and deliberate, like the practiced steps of a tango. The crowd's eagerness was infectious, and I felt an involuntary shiver of anticipation run down my spine. No matter how hard I tried to shut myself away from the world, it seemed that temptation would always find a way to slither into my sanctuary.

And then, at last, she appeared. DJ Ecciti stepped onto the stage, and it was as if the heavens themselves had opened up in tribute to her arrival. The crowd erupted in ecstatic cheers and applause, their cries of adulation piercing the sultry air like a chorus of angels heralding the second coming. It was a moment of pure, electric energy – a testament to the power she wielded over their hearts and minds.

I stood transfixed by the scene below me, unable to tear my gaze away as DJ Ecciti basked in the adoration of her followers, her every movement dripping with sensuality and grace. Her presence was intoxicating, a heady blend of desire and danger that threatened to consume me if I allowed it. But no matter how tempting the abyss might be, I knew that I must resist its pull, for there were darker forces at work that night, secrets that lay hidden beneath the veneer of celebration and excess.

As the music began to swell, filling the Piazza with its seductive rhythm, I found myself torn between the desire to flee from the darkness that threatened to engulf me and the temptation to succumb to it completely. But in the end, it was my duty that prevailed, a steadfast anchor in the stormy seas of my soul. And so, I remained there at my window, a silent witness to the unfolding drama, my heart heavy with the knowledge that the night's revelries would soon give way to sorrow and despair.

As the first few notes of her set drifted up to my window, I felt a shiver run down my spine – a frisson of anticipation that took me wholly by surprise. The darkness in my mind seemed to recede, if only for a moment, as I found myself drawn inexorably towards the allure of her music. It was as though she had cast a spell upon the entire state, ensnaring us all within her web of enchantment.

The pulsating beats of DJ Ecciti's music coursed through the air like an irresistible tide, washing over the teeming crowd and drawing them into its rhythmic embrace. From my vantage point in the cramped haven of my office, I could see how she deftly mixed the beats with the melodies, and between songs drank from an oversized mug advertising the main sponsor – the energy drink.

Sitting in the shadows of my office, I allowed myself to be carried away on the wings of her melody, feeling the weight of my previous case gradually lifting from my shoulders. For the first time in what felt like an eternity, I could breathe again, the sweet taste of freedom filling my lungs as I surrendered to the intoxicating power of her artistry.

But even amidst the heady throes of release, I could

not entirely escape the grip of my darker instincts. For every note that soared to the heavens, another seemed to burrow deep into the recesses of my soul, awakening long-dormant desires and kindling the embers of temptation that smoldered within. The music may have been a balm to my weary spirit, but it was also a force that threatened to consume me whole if I dared to let my guard down.

And so, as DJ Ecciti weaved her beguiling tapestry of sound, I remained rooted to my spot, a silent sentinel in the shadows. The knowledge that darkness still lurked beneath the surface of this glittering spectacle was an ever-present weight upon my conscience, a reminder that the line between good and evil was often as thin as the razor's edge.

It was in those moments of surrender to the swell of the music that I felt both most alive and most vulnerable, for I knew all too well the price one paid for straying from the path of righteousness. And as DJ Ecciti's set reached its crescendo, her music filling the Piazza like the breath of some divine being, her lithe form crumpled upon the stage, her enchanting melodies silenced as abruptly as a candle snuffed out by a cruel gust of wind. And in that breathless pause, I felt a perverse sense of relief - for the tempestuous sea of sound had at last been stilled, leaving only the faint echoes of its fury to haunt the dark recesses of my mind.

But this respite was short-lived. For as swift as a serpent's strike, the crowd's euphoric cheers curdled into gasps of shock, their rapturous cries transforming into the shrill keening of dismay. As if pulled by invisible strings, I found myself drawn to the window, my gaze riveted upon the scene unfolding below.

Through the haze of smoke and pulsating spotlights, I could make out the figures of those who had, but moments before, been dancing with wild abandon. Now they stood frozen in place, their bodies rigid with disbelief, as if caught in the spellbinding grip of Medusa's malevolent gaze. It was as though the world had been plunged into shadow, robbed of its vibrant colors and left with only the stark, unforgiving hues of truth and despair.

A cacophony of confusion and dismay enveloped the once euphoric atmosphere, as festival staff frantically scrambled onto the stage to attend to the fallen DJ Ecciti. From my perch above the chaos, I could see the kaleidoscope of colors transform into a swirling maelstrom of fear and uncertainty.

The pulsating rhythm that had served as the lifeblood of the festivities now lay silent, replaced by the staccato heartbeat of trepidation. The crowd, once united in their shared adoration for the enigmatic performer, found themselves fragmenting into disparate clusters, each one a microcosm of worry and hushed speculation.

As the first tendrils of panic began to creep through the sea of bodies below, I was reminded of an ancient Roman fresco I had once seen, depicting the fall of Pompeii – a moment frozen in time, where revelry and desire gave way to despair and destruction. It seemed somehow fitting that the same Italian soil now bore witness to another tragedy, one that would undoubtedly send tremors through the very foundations of the music world.

I allowed myself a fleeting reprieve from the turmoil outside my window, retreating deeper into the shadows of my lair. The room seemed to constrict around me, its once comforting embrace now suffocating. Though the darkness had been a sanctuary from the relentless energy of the festival, it had also served as a reminder of the sinister undercurrent that ran beneath the surface of such events – a world where temptation and power held sway, drawing unsuspecting souls into its seductive web.

And so, with a heavy heart and a mind filled with foreboding, I prepared myself to venture forth into the fray. I donned my coat like a suit of armor, feeling the weight of its fabric settle upon my shoulders, imbuing me with a sense of purpose. As I fastened the buttons, it felt as though I was sealing away the vulnerability that threatened to seep through the cracks in my hardened exterior.

Descending the narrow stairway leading to the Piazza della Libertà, I could feel the electric charge in the air, as though lightning had struck and left behind a residual current, prickling at my senses.

2

The once-festive atmosphere at Piazza della Libertá was now a somber symphony of murmuring voices and shuffling footsteps. The crowd began to dissipate, their faces painted with shock and despair as they whispered amongst themselves. DJ Ecciti's collapse on stage had cast a shadow over the festival in San Marino, her body crumpling like a discarded marionette. The air was thick with speculation; was it drugs that made her knees buckle? The sweltering heat? The weight of her own fame?

"Mi ha detto mio cugino che ha sentito un colpo," a woman muttered to her companion as they shuffled past me, her eyes wide with fear. Was it possible that someone had heard a gunshot? Could this be an act of terror?

I walked through the remnants of the festival scene, weaving my way through the bustling crowd. Like a dehydrated man at an oasis, I drank in the sights and sounds of the Piazza. My interest was piqued by the gossip that swirled around me like a sirocco wind, carrying seeds of truth and falsehood alike.

"Drugs," a man beside me said with certainty. "She was always so wild, you know?"

"Perhaps she simply couldn't handle the pressure," another chimed in, his voice dripping with condescension.

"Or maybe," an old woman interjected, a

conspiratorial gleam in her eye, "there are darker forces at play?"

The agitation of the crowd fueled my curiosity, igniting a fire within me that demanded answers. As a detective, it was my nature to seek out the truth, to separate the chaff from the wheat. And there was undoubtedly something worth uncovering in this cacophony of whispers and rumors.

My thoughts were consumed by the peculiarities of the night. The air hung heavy with uncertainty, and the once-jubilant atmosphere had been cast in shadow.

"Scusa," I murmured as my shoulder bumped into someone passing by.

"Ah!" a familiar voice cried as I bumped into a soft, fragrant form. I turned to see none other than Caterina, her raven hair cascading over her shoulders like a waterfall of midnight silk.

"Cara," I smiled, my heart skipping a beat at her sudden presence. "I didn't see you there."

"Clearly," she teased, her dark eyes dancing with mischief. "But I suppose I can forgive you, Ferro. After all, what happened tonight is rather...distracting."

"Indeed," I agreed, unable to resist her magnetic pull. "What are your thoughts on DJ Ecciti's collapse?"

"Such a tragedy," Caterina sighed, her lush lips curving into a pensive frown. "I can't help but wonder if it was more than just an accident."

"People have their theories," I conceded, thinking back to the whispers I'd heard earlier. "Drugs, heat stroke, even a gunshot..."

"Si, I've heard them all too," she said, her gaze

locked onto mine. "But I can't shake the feeling that something is lurking beneath the surface."

"Then perhaps we should dig deeper," I suggested, my curiosity ignited by her intuition. "Together."

"An intriguing proposition, Luigi," Caterina purred, her eyes gleaming with desire. "You always did know how to tempt me."

"Likewise, cara mia," I replied, the spark between us igniting into a blaze. And so, we began our journey home, each step echoing the growing intensity of our longing. The night air wrapped around us like a velvet cloak, whispers of intrigue and temptation carried on its gentle breeze.

As we reached her door, Caterina turned to face me, her eyes reflecting the desire we shared.

"Will you come in?" she asked, her voice sultry and inviting.

"With you, every time," I answered, my desire for her eclipsing all else. She led me inside, and our passion unfurled like the petals of a midnight rose, each caress an exploration of hidden depths and unspoken desires. We moved with a synchronicity forged by years of intimate knowledge, our bodies entwined like vines seeking the sun's touch.

*

We found refuge in the warm embrace of Caterina's apartment, a world removed from the chaos that had seized the festival. The weight of those events seemed to dissipate as we entered her dimly lit sanctuary, where electric anticipation hung in the air, pregnant with the promise of oblivion and surrender.

Caterina glided around with a seductive sway that defied the sultry night. I slowly pulled down the zipper at the back of her fifties-style dress. The sheer fabric of her lingerie whispered sinful promises against her skin, her sheer stockings a testament to sensuality and allure. I was transfixed, watching her transform into the embodiment of all my carnal desires – a temptress beckoning me to forget the dark world behind and indulge in much-needed pleasures.

The night unraveled like a dream, where time ceased to hold sway, and the only truth was the sensation of flesh against flesh. We wove a delicate tapestry of passion, each movement, each caress, banishing the memory of the festival into the void. The external world faded away, leaving only the intimate universe we had conjured.

As the first light of dawn seeped through the curtains, bathing our entwined forms in a gentle luminescence, Caterina and I lay in the serene aftermath. In the stillness, a profound understanding settled over me; we had found a way to transcend the storm, if only for the night. Our love was not just a haven but a force of resilience. Lying there, I gradually remembered the night before, the tumult of the festival and its tragic end. Caterina stirred beside me in bed, my fingers tracing patterns on her soft skin.

"Buongiorno," she murmured, her voice a sultry purr that sent shivers down my spine.

"Buongiorno, mia bella," I replied, pressing a tender kiss to her temple.

We disentangled ourselves from the cocoon of bed linen and each other, our movements languid and unhurried. As I watched Caterina dress, her delicate hands adjusting the straps of her dress, I couldn't help but think of how the fabric clung to her like a lover's embrace, echoing the contours of her body.

"Shall we go to the café for breakfast?" she asked, her eyes meeting mine, their depths promising more than just sustenance.

"Si, andiamo," I agreed, donning my shirt and jacket with practiced ease.

Stepping out into the San Marino morning, we made our way to a nearby café, its windows framed with ivy and adorned with wrought-iron tables. The sun kissed our faces as we sipped strong coffee, the hum of our desire still vibrating beneath our skins.

"Any news about DJ Ecciti?" Caterina inquired as I flipped through the morning's news.

"Nothing yet," I admitted, my thoughts drifting back to the unforgettable scene at Piazza della Libertà.

Suddenly, my phone buzzed, shattering the silence like glass against stone. It was an unknown number.

"Signor Ferro?" the voice on the other end said, urgency lacing every syllable. "It's Di Mauro, the direttore of SMTV who is responsible for the music festival. We need to talk."

"Parliamo," I replied.

"È morta!" he whispered, the director's tone both shocked and thrilled.

"DJ Ecciti is dead?" Caterina gasped as she overheard the conversation with her boss. "How?"

My fingers gripped the phone tightly as I sensed the weight of his words.

"Tell me more," I said, urging him to continue.

"Things are not progressing well with the gendarmerie's investigation," Di Mauro confessed, his tone heavy with frustration. "They're drowning in a sea of chaos and confusion, and the clock is ticking. The festival's reputation hangs in the balance, and we can't afford to let this tragedy define us."

"Nobody wants that," I agreed, my thoughts turning to the desolate faces in the crowd, the murmurs of suspicion and fear that had rippled through the Piazza della Libertá like a poisonous fog. "Does anyone suspect foul play, that her death was not natural?"

"Not in so many words," Di Mauro replied. "But that is what I want you to confirm. You possess a unique perspective, an uncanny ability to see beyond the surface and into the very heart of darkness. We need someone like you to uncover the truth behind DJ Ecciti's death."

"But the gendarmerie?" I hesitated, feeling the tendrils of doubt wrap themselves around my resolve. "This is too close to home."

"Exactly," Di Mauro countered, his voice firm with conviction. "You're part of the community and not bound by the same rules and expectations as the Gendarmerie. You can make inquiries they cannot. And time is of the essence, Signor Ferro. We need answers, and we need them now."

I looked at Caterina by my side; she had probably heard every word. She smiled and nodded. She knew that the seductive allure of the unknown beckoned me, tempting me to step beyond the comforting veil of ignorance and into the depths of San Marino's most hidden recesses.

"Very well," I acquiesced, feeling the weight of responsibility settle upon my shoulders like an exquisite Italian suit. "I will help you find the truth behind DJ Ecciti's death."

"Excellent," Di Mauro replied, relief evident in his voice. "Together, we must protect the festival's reputation and bring justice to those responsible for this heinous act."

As I ended the call, I knew the path before me was fraught with danger and temptation, but I also knew I could not turn away. For the sake of San Marino, for the memory of DJ Ecciti, and for SMTV and Caterina's employer, I would delve deep into the underbelly of this ancient city and unearth the secrets that lay buried within.

"Per San Marino," I whispered, raising my coffee cup in a salute.

Caterina squeezed my hand, her touch a balm against the darkness that threatened to engulf me.

"Signor Ferro, Signorina Curiale!" a voice called, shattering the spell that held us. A gendarme approached, his uniform both immaculate and imposing. "You must follow me to the station. We need to speak with you regarding last night's incident."

"Of course," I replied, my senses sharpening. It

seemed the San Marino Gendarmerie had been struggling to make progress in their investigation, hampered by the chaos and complexity of the festival setting. Witnesses were not scarce, but their accounts were fragmented and inconsistent, like pieces of a shattered mirror reflecting a distorted truth.

*

Within half an hour Caterina and I found ourselves ushered into the stark, fluorescent-lit corridors of the Gendarmerie's headquarters.

Commendante Mateo Capparoni greeted us, and without a word of explanation, we were separated. The silent command in Capparoni's gaze brooked no argument. I was led into a sparsely furnished room, the chill of the bare walls seeping into my bones.

The door closed with a definitive click behind me, and I took a seat across from Capparoni. His gaze that met mine was full of skepticism and doubt.

"Well, Ferro," he started, his tone accusatory. "I guess you spent the evening in your office, providing you with an unobstructed vantage point of the festival's area."

"Sure," I shrugged. "But I didn't watch that closely. I was mostly annoyed with the disturbance."

I recounted the events as well as I could, aware that every word, every inflection, was being scrutinized. The Commendante's eyes were relentless, missing nothing, pushing for details I struggled to recall. The atmosphere was charged with an unspoken accusation, and suspicion was heavy in the air.

"Ferro, we understand you watched when DJ Ecciti collapsed on stage. Can you tell us what you saw?" his question was sharp and probing.

"Indeed," I began, recalling the vivid scene. "I was drawn to my window by her transic melodies and pulsating rhythms, but I never saw anything that looked out of the ordinary – not that I have seen many music festivals …"

"And?" Capparoni probed. "What else?"

"She was dancing, or more jumping to the beats," I continued, the memory etching itself deeper into my mind. "She was mixing her songs – and, from what I can remember, she looked like she enjoyed what she was doing. And then she just dropped to the floor."

"Nothing else? Anyone moving about on stage? In the crowd?"

"Not that I noticed." I did my best to recall what I'd seen. "The crowd was dancing and singing along to her tunes, and the stage was empty as far as I can remember."

Capparoni muttered something and pushed out his chair, indicating the interview was over.

"There was one odd thing," I said as I stood. "She was drinking from an oversized mug."

"Si, that was part of the sponsor arrangements," Capparoni shrugged with half a smile.

"Commendante, why are you questioning us about this? Do you think her death was foul play?"

"Not at all," he reassured me. "Nothing suggests it was unnatural. We'll have to wait for the autopsy, but she was known to party, and you know what these artists are like, right?" He paused for a moment before he fixed me with his sharp gaze. "And Ferro, you won't get mixed up in this, will you? I suggest you let the authorities handle this!"

3

The festival grounds lay before me, a chiaroscuro of shadows and sorrows. The silence hung heavy in the air, wrapping around my shoulders like a cold embrace. I could almost hear the echoes of laughter and music that had filled these grounds just a few hours prior; now, they were as elusive as a woman's perfume on a summer night.

My eyes danced across the empty space, searching for any telltale signs of suspicious activity or potential clues. I knew that the key to unraveling the mystery surrounding DJ Ecciti's death lay hidden somewhere amidst these deserted stalls and abandoned tents.

As I wandered through the ghostly remnants of the festival, a small huddle of attendees caught my attention. They stood together, sharing their grief and sorrow, their voices soft and melodious like a tragic aria. I approached them cautiously, the gravel crunching underfoot, announcing my presence more loudly than I would have liked.

"Buongiorno," I began, my voice smooth as silk. "I am Luigi Ferro, a private investigator. I've been hired to look into the unfortunate passing of your beloved DJ Ecciti." I studied their faces, looking for any flicker of emotion that might betray a connection to the crime.

One young woman stepped forward, her eyes red-rimmed from tears. She wore a tight black dress, the fabric clinging to her body like a second skin.

"It's such a terrible loss," she whispered, her voice trembling. "DJ Ecciti was an icon, a true artist. Her music... it touched something deep inside all of us."

As she spoke, I noticed the others nodding in agreement, their eyes shining with unshed tears. It was clear that DJ Ecciti had been more than just an artist to these people; she had been a beacon of light in the darkness, a symbol of hope and rebellion.

One of the youths, his eyes alight with the passion of someone who had found profound inspiration in DJ Ecciti's music, leaned in closer.

"You know, it wasn't just the music itself, but how she created it. She had this unique approach to programming her beats, layering sounds in a way that nobody else did. It was like she was speaking a secret language through her music, one that resonated with us on a primal level."

Another, her hair dyed in vibrant colors that seemed to echo the vibrancy of Ecciti's music, chimed in excitedly, "Exactly! And her live sets—they were legendary. She'd somehow anticipated the crowd's energy, responding to it with her mixes in real time. It was as if she was conducting an orchestra of human emotions, guiding us through an unseen narrative."

"Her sets were like a dance between desire and temptation," another young man added, his voice thick with nostalgia. "She had an uncanny ability to weave together the most sensual beats and electrifying melodies. It was intoxicating, really."

I listened intently, piecing together the image of a woman who was not only a musical genius but a master of emotional alchemy. "So, it wasn't just about the music," I mused aloud, "but how she made you feel. Like she was reaching out, connecting with each of you personally."

The group gave a solemn nod, a collective acknowledgment of my understanding. It was clear DJ Ecciti had left an indelible mark on their lives, her artistry igniting a spark that continued to burn even in her absence.

"Thank you," I said softly, my eyes gravitating towards the young woman in the black dress once more. "Your words have given me a glimpse into the soul of DJ Ecciti, and they will not be forgotten. If you remember anything else, anything at all that might help me find the truth..."

I trailed off, leaving the question hanging in the air like a delicate thread. The group nodded silent goodbyes, their faces etched with the weight of their loss. They understood the importance of my task, the necessity of unmasking the darkness that had snuffed out the light of their beloved DJ.

As I turned away from them, the empty festival grounds stretched out before me once more, a vast canvas upon which to paint the unforgettable portrait of a life cut tragically short. My resolve hardened like steel, tempered by determination's heat and the slow burn of my desire for justice. For DJ Ecciti and for those who loved her, I would leave no stone unturned.

The afternoon sun bathed the Grand Hotel's facade in a warm embrace, casting shadows that played across its surface like forbidden lovers' fingertips. I stood outside, my eyes discreetly surveying the comings and goings of guests and staff, drinking in the atmosphere with a practiced thirst. The scent of jasmine and the faint murmur of laughter hung heavy in the air, tantalizing my senses and heightening the anticipation that simmered just beneath the surface.

My gaze flitted between faces, searching for any hint of discord among the harmonious throng. These were the people who had rubbed shoulders with DJ Ecciti, who had been privy to her innermost secrets and desires. Somewhere within their midst lurked the hidden hand that may have silenced her songs forever. It was my duty, my purpose, to unmask the truth that lay shrouded beneath layers of deceit and misdirection.

I entered the hotel lobby and found a seat on a plush black leather sofa. It would be a good and discrete lookout point over the flurry of activity, the crossroads for travelers from all walks of life.

Despite the bustle, she stood out like a beacon in the night. It wasn't just her appearance, which was striking, but the manner in which she navigated the space around her. She was poetry in motion, a symphony of grace and allure that captivated my attention. My eyes were drawn first to her legs, long and elegantly shaped, accentuated by the heels she wore with an ease that spoke of her confidence. They moved with a precision that hinted at a dancer's poise or perhaps just the natural gift of someone entirely comfortable in her own skin.

Her hair, dark as the midnight sky, cascaded over her shoulders in waves, framing a face that seemed as though it had been sculpted by divine hands. There was an ethereal quality to her beauty, one that transcended the mundane surroundings of the hotel lobby. The soft light played against her skin, highlighting the gentle curve of her neck, an expanse I found myself inexplicably drawn to. It spoke of vulnerability and strength in equal measure, a dichotomy that added layers to her allure.

As she moved, there was a languid grace to her every gesture, each one imbued with an innate sensuality that seemed to reach out, wrapping around me, igniting a fire within that I had long thought extinguished. It wasn't just her physical beauty that enthralled me; it was the air of authority that enveloped her, the unspoken power that lingered in her gaze, promising tales of passion and heartache.

My task at hand was forgotten. I was lost in my admiration, a silent observer content to marvel at this vision from afar when the unexpected happened. She noticed my gaze. It was a momentary connection, a spark that leaped across the distance between us, charged with an intensity that left my heart racing. Instead of the indifference I might have expected, a smile played upon her red lips, a silent invitation that emboldened her to approach.

As she neared, the world around me seemed to blur into insignificance, the background noise of the lobby fading into a distant murmur. Her presence was overwhelming, a force of nature that commanded my full attention.

"Is it the art of observation or mere curiosity that

has you so captivated?" she asked, her voice a melodic whisper that seemed to dance around me.

I was momentarily at a loss, caught between the desire to articulate my admiration and the fear of trespassing upon a moment that felt suspended in time.

"Perhaps a bit of both," I managed, "though I must confess, it's rare that such a sight so thoroughly captures my attention."

Her laughter was like music, a sound that seemed to resonate with the very core of my being.

"And here I thought I was the one doing the observing," she teased, a glint of mischief in her eyes. "Do you mind?" she said with a nudge towards the empty seat beside me.

I stood, gave her my hand, and welcomed her.

"My name is Ferro, Luigi Ferro," I greeted her.

"Sofia Ricci," she said as she sat down, carefully frapping the skirt around her delightful thighs.

"Signorina Ricci," I murmured, my voice low and intimate. "A pleasure to make your acquaintance."

"Ah, Signor Ferro," she replied, her voice like honey poured over crushed velvet. "I've heard whispers about you – a private investigator, is it?"

It was then that I realized this was not just a chance encounter; it was a meeting of two souls, each recognizing something in the other that defied explanation.

"Whispers can sometimes reveal more than shouts, Signorina," I said, my words laced with intrigue. "Did you know DJ Ecciti? A loss that has left a void in the hearts of many."

"I did," she sighed, her gaze drifting away as if chasing a memory. "I never knew her personally, but Aurelia, DJ Ecciti, was an icon to me — brilliant, unattainable, and gone all too soon."

"Did you ever notice anything off, any signs of discord or envy towards her from others? Anything that might suggest a deeper layer of animosity hidden beneath the surface adoration?" I probed, navigating the delicate waters of suspicion with the tact of a seasoned investigator.

Sofia Ricci paused, a flicker of contemplation crossing her features before she masked it with a cryptic smile. "I don't know," she finally replied, her voice laced with a hint of intrigue. "But in such a competitive arena, envy can often masquerade as admiration. It's a slippery slope, Ferro. One must tread carefully, for the divide between admiration and envy is as fragile as a silk stocking — easily admired, yet equally prone to tearing."

"True," I conceded, my gaze involuntary finding her gracious legs. "But sometimes, it is only by tearing through the veil that we can uncover the desires that lie hidden beneath."

"Ah, Signor Ferro," she whispered, her dark eyes glittering with untold secrets. "You are a dangerous man. But perhaps that is what makes you so... intriguing."

As her words hung seductively in the air, I felt the allure of temptation tugging at the edges of my resolve. Sofia Ricci embodied the very essence of desire, a living embodiment of power and seduction.

"Well, Signorina," I said, almost drowning in the depths of her beauty and sorrow, "this is a tragedy, indeed, that such a flame should be extinguished so soon."

"Tragedy?" Sofia echoed, a bitter smile playing at the corners of her mouth. "No, Signor Ferro. It is an injustice – a heresy, even. For someone to snuff out the light of such a radiant star... it is unfathomable."

"Indeed," I murmured, my mind racing with possibilities. Was Sofia merely a grieving friend or a beguiling femme fatale.

As I stood to leave, the weight of temptation lifted like a shroud.

"Thank you, Signorina," I said softly, trying to regain my balance and focus on my task. "Your insights have been most… illuminating. Do you think you can introduce me to some of her other friends? Colleagues?"

The question was met by a blank stare and a curious smile. "I cannot do your job, Ferro. But I hope you find the answers we all seek."

I ventured towards the hotel bar, where the DJ Marco Velluti held court among his eager acolytes. His laughter rang out like a clarion call, drawing me closer to the heart of the storm.

"Salute, Signor Velluti," I raised my glass in a toast, my gaze never leaving his face. "May the memory of DJ Ecciti live on in the hearts of all who loved her music."

"Salute," Marco echoed, his eyes narrowing with suspicion. "But tell me, Signore, who are you to speak of such things?"

"Merely a humble admirer," I replied, the lie rolling

smoothly off my tongue. "One who seeks solace in the company of those who shared her passion."

"Ah," Marco's lips curled into a predatory smile, as if he had sensed the deception beneath my words. "Then let us drink to our shared passions and the secrets that bound her fans together."

As the afternoon turned to early evening, I watched Marco like a hawk, searching for any chink in his armor, any whisper of malice or resentment that might betray the darkness within. Yet even as I sifted through the glittering shards of conversation that filled the room, I could not escape the tempting lure of Sofia Ricci – her sultry voice like a siren's song, drawing me ever deeper into the murky depths of desire and deceit.

The hotel bar was filled with an eerie energy, as if unseen spirits were lurking in the shadows and dancing across the polished marble floor. The sad sorrow of other fans could penetrate the bar, but it held an enigmatic glow that made me think of a strange, otherworldly forcefield.

That potent vision strengthened my senses as I approached the enigmatic figure of Marco Velluti.

"Ah, the tragedy of losing such a talented soul," I murmured, feigning a fan's sorrow as I clinked my glass with his in a somber toast. "DJ Ecciti's music truly spoke to the very depths of one's being."

"Indeed," Marco mused, his eyes narrowing behind a veil of suspicion. "And yet, even the brightest stars must eventually fade away, leaving only darkness in their wake."

I studied his face closely as he spoke, searching for

any telltale signs of guilt or unease that might betray his true nature. Yet beneath the mask of grief and camaraderie, I detected nothing more than the cold, calculated indifference of a predator sizing up its prey.

"Perhaps," I ventured cautiously, "it is in that darkness that we find our true selves – stripped bare of all pretense, raw and exposed in the unforgiving light of the truth."

"Ah, but who among us can ever claim to truly know themselves?" Marco replied, his voice tinged with the bitter irony of one who has plumbed the depths of his own soul only to find it wanting. "For are we not all mere pawns in the grand game of life, subject to the whims of fate and the machinations of those who seek to control us?"

I took a few steps back and wondered if it was possible to get close to these people without telling them who I was and what I had been engaged to do.

"Luca Bianchi," I heard a voice murmur at my side. "You know, her manager."

Intrigued, I cast my gaze surreptitiously toward the source of the conversation – two festival-goers, their faces animated by a mixture of curiosity and disdain as they discussed the enigmatic figure whose very name seemed to evoke an aura of danger and mystery.

"I heard he pushed Ecciti further than she could take it," the other confided, his words weaving a sinister tapestry of deceit and betrayal that ensnared my thoughts like a spider's web.

"Could it be?" I pondered silently, my heart quickening with the thrill of the chase. I made a mental note to talk with that manager as I turned towards the two guys.

"Ah, ragazzi," I greeted them before trying a blatant lie. "I couldn't help but hear your conversation. You wouldn't think her boyfriend could? I've heard rumors..."

"Rumors about what, man?" the taller one replied with a smirk. "He was still in love with her, worshiped the ground she walked on even after the terrible breakup."

"Don't speak ill about the dead," the shorter one said hesitantly, his voice thick with emotion. "Ecciti was a true artist and her death... it has left a void in our hearts that no amount of music can ever fill."

"Such a tragedy," I agreed, "Do you think Marco Velutti can fill her space?"

"He is good; I like him," the tall one replied.

"But it's hard to believe he can fill Ecciti's shoes," the shorter one filled in.

I decided to steer the conversation back to the enigmatic figure whose name had piqued my interest earlier. "And to think that there are those who whisper of perilous dealings and the involvement of Luca Bianchi..."

"Luca Bianchi?" the taller one echoed, his brow furrowing in consternation. "He may be a shady character, but what could he possibly have to gain by Ecciti's death?"

"Ah, that is the question, isn't it?" I mused, watching their reactions closely as I planted the seeds of doubt and suspicion. "But perhaps there are other, darker motives at play... Do you know where I can find the ex-lover?"

"Giancarlo Rossi?" the shorter one asked. "I heard he is curled up with grief in his hotel room. He won't come out."

*

As I approached Giancarlo's hotel room, I paused for a moment in the corridor that breathed more luxury than a simple passage to the rooms. It had been easy enough to get the room number; the receptionist was a childhood schoolmate, and I had the feeling she would still do anything for me.

I knocked on the door, steeling myself for the torrent of emotion that would follow. When the door opened, there stood Giancarlo, his eyes haunted by the ghosts of memories past, his hands trembling as they clutched the doorframe.

"Signor Rossi," I began, my voice gentle yet insistent, "I am Luigi Ferro, a private investigator looking into the tragic death of your beloved Aurelia. May I come in? I believe we have much to discuss."

The air in the dimly lit hotel room was thick with the scent of incense, weaving an intoxicating spell around my senses. Giancarlo eyed me warily, his chiseled features softened by the flickering candlelight that danced like fiery sprites upon the walls.

"Sure, Signor Ferro," he said, stepping aside to allow me entrance into his sanctuary of sorrow. "I hope you understand the pain I feel at this moment."

I nodded solemnly, taking in the array of mementos and keepsakes that adorned the room – a shrine to a love taken too soon from this world. I settled into the plush velvet armchair and began my delicate inquiry. "Giancarlo, you and Aurelia shared a passionate bond, one that many envied. Did her meteoric rise to fame ever cause... friction between you?"

He hesitated, his fingers dancing nervously over the rim of his wine glass. "At times, yes," he admitted, his voice barely above a whisper. "It was difficult to see her adored by so many, knowing that I alone was not enough to keep her satisfied."

"Did this dissatisfaction ever manifest itself in anger? Perhaps resentment?" I pressed, watching the shadows playing across his face, betraying the turmoil within.

"Anger? Yes," he confessed, his voice cracking with emotion. "But never towards her. Only towards myself for not being the man she deserved. But I would never harm her, Signor Ferro? My love for her burns as brightly now as it ever did."

I let his words hang in the air, swirling amongst the thoughts that licked at the corners of the room. I ventured further into the shadows that could cling to Aurelia's person.

"Apart from her music, were there other dealings Aurelia had? Any known enemies?" I asked, watching him closely for any flicker of insight.

At first, Giancarlo was in shock, genuinely disbelieving that such a question could be pertinent. "Enemies? Aurelia? She was loved, admired... who could possibly..." His voice trailed off, the idea of foul play painting a stark, unsettling picture that he seemed reluctant to consider.

But then, as if the mention of enemies had loosened a lock within him, he leaned forward, a hesitant urgency in his tone. "An investor, a billionaire whose name she never mentioned to me, approached her," he said, his gaze lost somewhere between the memories and the pain they brought. "This investor was interested in her work, not just the music, but the technology behind it. Aurelia had been developing some kind of software algorithm for music production, something revolutionary. It was all quite secretive."

His revelation hinted at complexities I hadn't anticipated, suggesting Aurelia's talents and aspirations had indeed transcended her musical achievements. This investor, this shadowy figure with vast resources, could be a vital piece of the puzzle, possibly even the motive lurking behind her tragic end.

"Thank you, Giancarlo," I said, standing and offering a handshake to the man who had unwittingly broadened the scope of my inquiry. "Your information has been invaluable. I may need to speak with you again. Will you be staying in town?"

"At least till the authorities are done," he replied with a sad nod.

I couldn't help but feel a pang of sympathy for the man. His eyes were bloodshot and baggy, his hair unkempt and shaggy. It was clear he had been through a lot.

I felt he was holding back something he didn't want to tell me. But what could it be?

With every step I took away from Giancarlo's room, I felt that this investigation did not move at all. Her fans seemed to love her and grieve her. Marco Velluti, the rival DJ, barely concealed his jealousy toward DJ Ecciti, but could it be merely a facade, a mask worn to protect him?

And then there was Giancarlo, the grieving ex-lover. The pain etched onto his face had been raw and visceral, but even the most passionate love can turn sour, becoming a poison that infects the heart, leading to the most heinous of acts.

The summer night enveloped me like a lover's embrace, heavy with desire and anticipation. The music festival organizers had decided to keep it going, but in a slower, more subtle tone, and my footsteps echoed through the quiet streets.

"Buona sera, detective," a voice whispered from the shadows, as smooth as silk and twice as seductive. I turned to find Sofia Ricci emerging from the darkness, her eyes alight with a fire that burned deep within her soul, the moonlight casting a sultry glow on her olive skin. Her gaze caught mine and held my eyes prisoner, daring me to look away. I couldn't. With every step I took toward her, the magnetic pull intensified, drawing me into her orbit.

"Ah, Signorina Ricci," I replied, my voice steady despite the surge of emotions coursing through my veins. "It's a pleasure to see you again, though I must admit, I am surprised to find you here."

"Should a woman not be allowed to walk the streets in the dark?" she asked, her lips curving into a smile that could melt even the coldest of hearts. "Or is it simply that my presence threatens to upend your carefully laid plans?"

"Nothing so dramatic, I assure you," I said, my gaze never leaving hers.

"Then why don't you let me follow you?" she offered, stepping closer. The scent of her perfume was intoxicating, a heady blend of jasmine and danger that sent shivers down my spine.

"Non posso," I murmured, my mind racing with a thousand possibilities, each more treacherous than the last. "This path is mine to walk alone."

"Very well," she conceded, her voice tinged with disappointment and something else, something I couldn't quite place. "But can't a woman ask for some company in her quest for pleasure?"

Her words were laced with temptation, weaving a web of desire that threatened to ensnare me. But

I couldn't let myself be distracted from my quest for the truth—not now, not when I was on my way to the depths of a dark case.

"Believe me, Signorina, I am not immune to the allure of nocturnal delights. But my heart is heavy with the weight of an unsolved mystery, and I fear it leaves little room for anything else."

As I turned to leave, Sofia's hand shot out to grasp my arm, her grip firm yet tender as she pulled me close. "Be careful, Ferro," she whispered, her breath warm against my cheek. "Your dedication to your work is admirable, but even the most steadfast detective needs a moment to indulge his desires. Life is short, after all."

Her lips curved into a knowing smile, and for a fleeting second, I found myself teetering on the edge of temptation. The sultry night air swirled around us like a cloak of secrecy, whispering promises of pleasure and escape.

"Perhaps you're right," I conceded, my resolve wavering under the weight of Sofia's hypnotic gaze. "But some mysteries refuse to be left unsolved, and their siren song is too powerful to resist."

"Then let me be your siren, detective," she whispered, the heat of her breath brushing against my ear. "And perhaps, in our dance of desire, we can uncover secrets more intoxicating than any you've ever known."

I was wary, acutely aware of the game she played. Sofia was a master of manipulation, her allure a weapon she wielded with precision. Yet, tonight, I was reluctant to engage in our usual dance of wits and wills.

Her offer was tempting, dangerously so. Information

was a currency I could never afford to turn down outright, not with the stakes so high. But it was Sofia herself who presented the most significant risk. Her presence was a labyrinth, easy to enter but potentially impossible to leave.

Despite my instincts screaming caution, curiosity — that eternal weakness of mine — began to chip away at my resolve.

"And why would you offer me this, Sofia? What's in it for you?"

She laughed, a sound that seemed to wrap around me, a tactile caress in the cool night air. "Oh, Ferro, always so direct. But I'm not here to get anything. I'm offering you a gift — all I ask in return is your company...for an unforgettable night."

She took my arm, guiding me through the winding streets toward her hotel, a place that promised both revelations and regret. Each step was a pact with potential damnation, but the detective in me couldn't resist the lure of hidden truths, even if they were offered by the likes of Sofia Ricci.

As we entered her opulent hotel room, the part of me that acknowledged the danger of intertwining my fate with hers, even for a night, vanished. Sofia had set the stage for a night that promised to be unforgettable, and I, willingly or not, had accepted the invitation to play my part.

Her eyes locked with mine, and she brushed her hair back with one hand, revealing her bare, slender shoulder. In the dim light, each revealing layer seemed to come alive, revealing more of the woman beneath the glamorous veneer.

My gaze was transfixed, helpless in the face of her seductive dance of desire as each piece of clothing fell to the floor. The first layer was a dress, followed by a lace bra that matched her panties, inviting me into the realm of her secret fantasies.

Sofia's every movement was deliberate, each shrug of a shoulder, each parting of her legs revealing hidden areas of her body. I watched as she peeled off each layer of her undergarments, her body responding to the erotic dance she created. With each touch, with each tug of her clothes, emotions swirled around us, the anticipation thick and electric.

The sight of her flawless skin, the luscious curves, and the desire that seemed to radiate from her core made my blood race in response. It was a display of seduction unlike any I'd ever seen, her body's language one full of raw desire and sensual pleasures.

By the time she stood before me, clad only in her shoes and stockings, I'd been drawn into a sexual tension I was powerless to resist. From the first brush of her hair to the last glimpse of her undergarments, Sofia's slow, enticing striptease created a world of desire and longing, a hidden world waiting to consume me. The urgency in her gaze was intoxicating, a stark reminder of the promises she'd made earlier in the night.

As she pulled me towards the bed, she swayed her hips, each step gracefully sensuous. The deliberate sway of her shoulders added an erotic rhythm to her dance, drawing me in as though pulled by some unseen force. But it wasn't just the sway of her hips or the silk sheen of her skin that captivated me; it was the burning need in her eyes, the languid sensuality of her movements, and the intensity of the longing she channeled her way.

As we reached the bed, Sofia pushed me down slowly, her gaze never leaving mine, as she straddled my hips. The cool touch of the sheet against my back was in stark contrast to the fire she was slowly building within me.

Her fingers brushed against my chest, her touch gentle yet assertive, as she leaned in for a kiss. The intensity of our connection was palpable, the exchange of passion converging into one electrifying moment. Her lips were soft and supple, her kiss tender yet demanding, conflating my reason and desire.

As the kiss deepened, my hands roamed her body, caressing every delicate curve and muscle hidden beneath her skin. The silky smoothness of her skin under my touch was a contrast to the heated fervor simmering between us. It felt like every touch ignited a sensual spark, the culmination of desire and sensuality, stoking a fire she wanted me to tend.

She moaned softly, her hips gyrating in response to my touch. The feeling of her warmth against my skin, the sway of her hips, the flush of her cheeks, she was an ethereal concoction of sensuality and desire, a heady rush of emotions that I felt powerless to resist.

With each passing second, the intensity between us grew more intense, the passion more visible. It was an intoxicating dance of desire and urgency, each touch bringing us closer to a point of no return.

In the midst of the blaze she was creating, I couldn't help but wonder if this was a good idea. I was drawn into a world of temptation, desire, and mystery, a world where the lines of right and wrong were blurry, and reality seemed but a distant memory. But as I succumbed to her gaze and my body followed her cues, I realized that perhaps this was an aspect of the case I couldn't solve by myself. Could this encounter offer hidden keys to understanding the case? Or would it only cloud my judgment?

Regardless, as we were drawn into a whirlwind of sensuality and passion, the truth of the night remained a mystery, one waiting for the dawn to reveal.

*

The morning sun crept through the sliver of a gap between velvet curtains, casting a delicate golden beam upon the tangled limbs and tousled sheets. A symphony of birdsong filtered in from the streets below, their melodies weaving through the quietude of Sofia Ricci's room.

I stirred beneath the exquisite silken linens, my body still humming with the echoes of last night's passions. Yet, as I gazed upon the breathtaking visage of the woman who lay beside me, I could not help but feel a nagging curiosity gnawing at the corners of my mind – for what secrets did this enigmatic beauty harbor amidst the shadows of San Marino?

"Buongiorno, Detective," she purred, her voice a

sultry caress that sent shivers down my spine. "Do you see anything you like?"

"Very much so," I smiled, the satisfaction of our shared desires tempered by the lingering uncertainty about her true intentions. "But there is still much to uncover."

"Ah, ever the sleuth," she teased, tracing the contours of my chest with her slender fingertips. "But beware, Ferro: sometimes the truth we seek can be as treacherous as the temptations we resist."

Before I could respond, the shrill ring of my phone sliced through the intimate haze, its discordant notes shattering the fragile serenity of our post-coital reprieve. I reached for the device, my heart pounding in anticipation as Di Mauro's name flashed across the screen.

"Pronto," I commanded tersely, my eyes never leaving Sofia's inscrutable gaze.

"DJ Ecciti's death was no accident, Ferro," Di Mauro hissed, each word laden with the weight of grim revelation. "The Gendarmerie's findings are wrong. It's murder."

"Are you certain?" I asked, my pulse quickening from the surge of adrenaline coursing through my veins.

"Without a doubt," he affirmed. "And you must be careful – there are those who would do anything to keep this truth buried."

"Of course," I replied, with a feeling of uncertainty for the path that lay before me. As I ended the call, I turned towards Sofia, her eyes dark and impenetrable.

A veil of disbelief hung over me like a silken shroud, Di Mauro's words echoing in my ears as I attempted to process the revelation. My fingertips grazed the phone's chilled metal. The screen was black and unyielding, a mirror of the unfathomable depths that awaited me in this case.

"Murder," I whispered, the word an insidious caress upon my tongue. It was a waltz I had danced before, yet never with a partner so enigmatic, so alluring as the elusive DJ Ecciti. Her life, her secrets, her very essence – they taunted me from beyond the grave, daring me to unravel the tangled threads that bound her to this mortal coil.

"Is everything alright, Ferro?" Sofia's sultry and melodic voice wound its way around my senses like the tendrils of smoke that curled languidly through the air.

"Si, tutto bene," I replied nonchalantly, unwilling to share the gravity of the situation with this bewitching woman who held a tempest of desire and deception within her. "Something came up, and I have to run."

I retrieved my shirt, the fabric cool against my heated skin, and slipped it on with practiced ease. My thoughts, however, were elsewhere – tangled in the web of intrigue that now surrounded DJ Ecciti's death.

"Arrivederci, Sofia," I murmured, my voice laced with the promise of future rendezvous despite my growing conviction that she held more than lustful secrets within her beguiling embrace.

"Addio, detective," she replied, the corners of her lips curling upward in a knowing smile. As I closed the door behind me, I dialed Capparoni's number, impatient for answers that would shed light on this dark mystery.

"Ah, Ferro," he gruffly greeted me, his voice betraying the weight of countless sleepless nights spent combing through evidence. "You're looking for more information on DJ Ecciti, yes?"

"Si," I replied, my resolve unwavering as I pressed him for details. "What did her autopsy reveal? Did she have any drugs in her system or anything unusual?"

"Nothing," Capparoni sighed, frustration lacing his words. "No drugs, no abnormalities. It's as if she just stopped. There is no rhyme or reason."

"Then you must dig deeper," I declared, my mind racing with frustration. "A young woman like that don't just drop dead for no reason.""

"Sometimes they do," he replied. " The report was definite." The conversation fell silent as neither of us knew what to add.

As I ended the call, I gazed upon the sun-drenched streets of San Marino, their secrets beckoning me like the outstretched arms of a siren. I had made a promise to my client, Di Mauro of SMTV, to delve deeper and find the truth, but what intrigued me was what made Di Mauro so sure her death was not natural.

"DJ Ecciti," I whispered, my voice a solemn vow to the memory of a woman who had touched so many lives. Her music was a symphony of passion and pain.

5

The SMTV offices, a maze of glass and buzzing lights felt sterile as I walked its corridors. Each step echoed, a solitary beat against the background hum until I reached direttore Di Mauro's door. It was ajar, either an invitation or a challenge. Pushing it open, I found him silhouetted against the cityscape, posture rigid with anticipation or maybe apprehension.

"Di Mauro," I greeted him, my voice steady. "You insist Ecciti's death wasn't accidental. Why? What makes you so certain?"

Umberto Di Mauro rose from behind his desk with an ever-present grin. Towering over most, he was impeccably dressed in a three-piece linen suit, the shirt beneath gleaming white, set off by a striking red tie. Gray grazed his temples, adding distinction to his clean-shaven face, which bore the warm patina of sun-kissed skin.

His eyes flickered momentarily. "Ferro, you know. Ecciti wasn't just talented; she was a force. Her music, her presence... it stirred something deep. But not always good."

Silence fell between us, heavy and expectant.

He sighed, the sound heavy with unspoken truths. "There were rumblings. Discontent and jealousy where there should have been admiration. Ecciti was a beacon, but beacons cast shadows."

"And in those shadows, you suspect foul play?" I pushed, my skepticism barely hidden.

"Exactly." Di Mauro moved from his desk, his movements deliberate. "Her genius wasn't just art; it was innovation. She was on the verge of something big, something disruptive. That didn't sit well with everyone."

His words wove through my mind, implications dark and tangled. "Her breakthrough, her success, made her a target… and who would you suspect?"

He nodded, grim confirmation. "In this industry, everyone is as much a suspect as a victim. Whom have you talked to so far?"

I mentioned the DJ Marco Velluti, her ex-boyfriend Giancarlo Rossi, and some nameless fans, but I intentionally did not name Sofia Ricci.

"So, you haven't met her manager yet?" Di Mauro grunted.

*

The heavy oak door to Luca Bianchi's sanctuary beckoned with a silent promise, a veiled secret waiting in the shadow of its polished veneer. I adjusted the cuff of my sleeve, the fine Italian fabric a subtle armor against the deceit that clung to this investigation like a second skin. My fingers curled around the brass handle, cool and unyielding, as I steeled myself for the encounter.

"So, you are Ferro," Dj Ecciti's manager quivered like a plucked string as he emerged from the abyss of his office, "I wasn't expecting you so soon." His attempt at composure could fool a layman, but not me. I caught the flicker of his eyes, darting to the corners of the room, seeking refuge in shadows that weren't there.

"Buongiorno," I said, my voice low and steady. As I crossed the threshold, the hairs on the back of my neck stood on end as if an electric charge coursed through the air. Then, I caught it—a scent as intoxicating as it was enigmatic like the memory of a lover long gone but never forgotten. He gestured towards the chair opposite his cluttered desk, a pitiful stage for innocence where none resided.

"Please, have a seat," he offered, the words slipping from his lips with the oily ease of a practiced liar. I obliged, the chair creaking under the weight of truth yet to be unearthed. His hands betrayed him, fidgeting with the edge of the blotter, betraying a symphony of nerves.

"Let's not waste time with pleasantries, shall we?" I suggested, my gaze locked onto his. "We both know why I'm here."

"Of course," he murmured, his voice barely rising above the hum of the tourists that bled through the open window. San Marino's eternal pulse was a backdrop to our grim tableau, a reminder of the countless secrets buried beneath cobblestone streets.

"DJ Ecciti... Aurelia..." he began but halted, his Adam's apple bobbing in a desperate swallow. I watched the struggle play across his features, a man clinging to the remnants of his resolve.

"Her death was untimely," I continued, filling the

silence he left gaping wide, "and you're going to help me understand why."

"Signor Ferro," he started again, this time a hint of steel lining his tone, a futile shield raised against the onslaught of truth. "I assure you, I am at a loss as much as anyone."

"Assurances are currency for fools," I countered, my words slicing through the haze of his fear. "And I am no fool."

"Of course, Signor Ferro," he finally croaked. "I'll tell you what I know."

"Tell me," I began, leaning forward, my gaze locked on his eyes. "What can you tell me about DJ Ecciti's recent activities? Who were her friends, her enemies? Did she have any... conflicts within the industry?"

The manager shifted uncomfortably in his seat, his shirt shimmering like liquid silver. He licked his lips, the tip of his tongue flickering out like a serpent's, tasting the secrets he held within.

"DJ Ecciti... she was, uh, very popular, both professionally and personally," he stammered, sweat beading on his brow despite the coolness of the room. "She had many admirers – men and women alike. But there were also those who envied her success, who coveted what she had."

"Such as?" I prompted.

"Other DJs, promoters, even some of the club owners," the manager replied, swallowing hard. "They wanted a piece of the pie, you see – a slice of her fame, her talent, her power."

"Power," I mused, letting the word roll off my tongue

like a delectable morsel. "And what of Aurelia? Did she possess any… particular power that might have made her a target?"

The manager hesitated, his eyes darting around the room as if searching for an escape from the truth he was about to reveal.

"She was… influential," he finally admitted. "Her music, her style, had the power to make or break careers, to open doors that were closed to others. But that's all I can say, Signor Ferro. I don't know anything more."

"Very well," I acquiesced, allowing the shadows of suspicion to recede from my gaze, if only for a moment. "Let us turn our attention, then, to the relentless rhythm of her career – the ceaseless beat of gigs that took her across the length and breadth of Europe, from the sun-drenched shores of Sicily to the mist-shrouded moors of Scotland." My fingers traced the edge of the polished desk, their touch as light and fleeting as the whisper of a lover's breath. "Were you not concerned that you were pushing her too far, too fast? That the delicate flame of her talent might flicker and fade beneath the crushing weight of your ambition?"

Luca Bianchi shifted uncomfortably in his chair, the fabric of his trousers rustling like the wings of a restless dove. "Signor Ferro, I... I only wanted the best for Aurelia. She was destined for greatness, and it was my duty, my honor, to help her achieve it." His eyes met mine, a flicker of defiance dancing within their depths. "Her passion for music was insatiable, her desire to share her gift with the world unquenchable.

I did what I thought was best for her career, always mindful of her needs and wishes."

"Ah, but a career can be fickle," I countered, my words as smooth and dark as the richest espresso. "It can seduce us with sweet promises of pleasure and power, only to ensnare our souls in a web of deceit and torment." My gaze pierced through him, revealing the secrets lurking within his heart's recesses. "You must ask yourself, Bianchi—were you truly serving Aurelia's best interests or merely your own?"

The scent still lingered, its tendrils caressing the air like a lover's whisper, teasing at the edges of my consciousness. It was familiar yet elusive – a fleeting memory that danced just beyond the grasp of my outstretched fingertips, taunting me with the promise of revelation.

"Signor Ferro," the manager stammered, his voice a tremulous crescendo of fear and desire. "I have told you all I know. Please, let me be."

"Your reluctance speaks volumes, Bianchi," I said, my voice low and silky. "But your eyes reveal even more." I leaned in closer, my gaze locked onto his like a predator stalking its prey. "Tell me, what is it that you're hiding? What secret lies buried beneath the surface?"

The manager squirmed, beads of sweat glistening on his brow. His discomfort was palpable, almost intoxicating. I could feel the power coursing through my veins, a heady thrill that sent shivers of anticipation dancing down my spine.

"Alright," he whispered, defeated by my unrelenting stare. "There was... something else. Something big."

"Go on," I encouraged, my pulse quickening at the prospect of unearthing yet another layer of this twisted mystery.

"Aurelia had been working on a new software algorithm for her music," Luca Bianchi revealed, visibly trembling under the weight of his confession. "It was groundbreaking—unlike anything we've ever seen before. It would have revolutionized the entire industry."

"An innovation so profound that others would kill to possess it?" I mused, savoring the rich irony of such a compelling idea.

"Unlikely," he replied, his voice barely audible. "But other DJs, promoters, even tech companies – they all wanted a piece of it. They were willing to do whatever it took to get their hands on it."

"Tell me more about this algorithm," I demanded, my curiosity piqued by the allure of forbidden knowledge.

"I don't know much about the technical details," he admitted, his eyes pleading for forgiveness. "But I heard rumors that it could manipulate sound in ways never thought possible – bending frequencies, melding genres, even controlling the very emotions of the listener."

"Now we're getting somewhere," I murmured, my thoughts racing with the implications of such a powerful tool. "Did Aurelia share this algorithm with anyone? Was there anyone she trusted enough to reveal her secret?"

"Only me," the manager confessed, his voice laced

with guilt and regret. "But I never thought... I never imagined that it would lead to this."

"Know this, Bianchi," I intoned, the weight of my words bearing down upon him like the crushing force of history itself. "I will not rest until I have uncovered the truth until I have brought justice to Aurelia and torn the mask from the face of her killer. No stone shall be left unturned, no secret left unexplored – for that is my sworn duty, my sacred calling."

As I turned to leave, my thoughts churned like the turbulent waters of the Tiber, swirling with questions, suspicions, and the ever-present specter of desire. For beneath this tangled intrigue lay a truth as ancient and powerful as Italy itself, a truth that would test the limits of my courage, cunning, and resolve. And I knew, without a doubt, that I would stop at nothing to claim it.

*

The sun had started to set over the roofs, casting long shadows that stretched like fingers across San Marino's ancient cobblestones, caressing the walls that whispered tales of love, lust, and betrayal.

"DJ Ecciti," I murmured beneath my breath as I left the manager Luca Bianchi's office. "A life cut tragically short – but why?"

My thoughts whirled like the delicate eddying of a dancer's skirt, brushing against the tantalizing possibility of motives far more sinister than a mere personal vendetta. Was it possible that her murder had been orchestrated as part of a grander scheme? That her death was not the result of passion or jealousy but a calculated move to seize control of the innovative music technology she had developed?

And then I knew where I'd smelt that alluring scent before. It was in a hotel room not long ago, and I realized I had things to do. I straddled my trusty Vespa and returned to my office in Piazza della Libertá.

When I returned to my office, the last thing I expected was to find the door unlocked, a silent herald of the unexpected. The click of the lock opening with the turn of my key had always been a reassurance, a finality to the day's chaos.

Pushing the door open with a caution born of instinct, I was unprepared for the sight that greeted me. Sofia Ricci, an enigma wrapped in the guise of seduction, sat atop my desk, her presence as deliberate as it was disarming. The sunlight spilled through the blinds, casting her in a chiaroscuro that accentuated the deliberate hike of her skirt, revealing sheer stocking tops—a blatant challenge to my professionalism.

My initial reaction was a cocktail of disturbance and intrigue.

"Signorina Ricci," I began, my tone colder than an alpine storm, "to what do I owe this... unexpected pleasure?"

Her laughter, a melody woven with danger and allure, filled the space between us. "Ferro," she purred, her voice a brushstroke of intimacy, "always straight to business. But sometimes, business can be... pleasurable."

I remained by the door, an island in the storm of

her charm. "Let's talk business then. Your connection with Luce Bianchi—what's your angle?"

As I questioned her, pressing for the truth behind her involvement with key players in this mystery, Sofia's facade of flirtation began to crumble, revealing glimpses of her true intentions. She leaned forward, the game of seduction giving way to one of strategy.

"I've been planning to invest in Ecciti's software," she confessed, her admission slicing through the charged atmosphere. "That algorithm—it's revolutionary."

"So, you are the unknown investor? The billionaire?" I asked, narrowing the distance between us with a few measured steps. The room seemed to contract, the air thick with the revelation hanging between us. Ecciti's software was morphing into the epicenter of intrigue, attracting key players from the shadows into a dangerous dance. Sofia's involvement underscored the algorithm's worth and the peril it harbored.

Sofia's smile was a blend of pride and secrecy as she nodded. "Yes, Ferro, I am. My interactions with Aurelia were discreet, consisting of a series of clandestine meetings and hidden correspondences. I saw the potential in her vision and the revolutionary impact it could have on the world. We were planning to make the software public, to change the industry forever."

Her revelation added depth to the narrative unfolding before me. Sofia Ricci, far from just a seductress or a mere player in the shadows, was a visionary seeking to elevate Ecciti's creation to its deserved pedestal.

"Aurelia and I shared a dream," Sofia continued, her

voice softening with a hint of melancholy. "But before we could bring our plans to fruition, she was taken from us. Her untimely death left the project in limbo, the software's whereabouts now a mystery."

The pieces of the puzzle were aligning, yet each revelation only served to deepen the enigma. Sofia's admission of her secret partnership with Aurelia cast her in a new light, transforming my understanding of her motives and her role in this intricate web of secrets and ambitions.

"And I want you, Ferro, to help me find it," she concluded, her resolve crystallizing as she slid off my desk.

I was already knee-deep in this investigation, navigating a web that seemed to entangle further with each revelation. Yet Sofia's offer of assistance presented an opportunity.

"I'm already on this case, as you know. But your… assistance could prove useful," I conceded, the detective in me recognizing the advantage of having eyes and ears in places I couldn't reach alone.

Sofia moved towards me, the motion all grace and calculated allure, yet her eyes held a new light—a blend of respect and challenge. "Then consider me your… partner in this endeavor," she said, extending her hand, not in seduction, but in alliance.

As she departed, leaving a trail of intrigue in her wake, I sat at my desk, the weight of the investigation pressing down with renewed intensity. With her connections and willingness to invest in Ecciti's creation, Sofia Ricci had become an unlikely ally in the tangled mystery of the DJ's untimely demise and the hunt for her revolutionary software.

The evening had fallen outside my window, the city a labyrinth of light and shadow. Within these walls, the lines between professional detachment and the lure of the unknown blurred. Sofia's visit had disturbed the equilibrium of my solitude, but it had also injected a new dynamism into the case.

Yes, I was up to my knees in this investigation, but now I had Sofia Ricci, with her resources and insights, albeit for her own ends. The path ahead was fraught with complication and peril, yet the detective in me couldn't deny the thrill of the hunt, the allure of uncovering secrets meant to remain shrouded in darkness.

As the city slept, I poured over my notes, Sofia's information weaving into the fabric of my case. The mystery of Ecciti's software and the motives of those circling it was a puzzle I was determined to solve. With every player that emerged from the shadows, the stakes climbed higher, but so did my resolve to uncover the truth.

6

Under cover of the morning's shadow, the sun's attempt to illuminate Marco Velluti's dark basement studio was thwarted; its beams denied entry into this sanctum of creativity and nocturnal musings. Within the studio, the air was thick with the scent of anise and tobacco, an aroma that now served as an extension of the persona I had carefully assumed. Today, I was no longer Luigi Ferro, private investigator, but instead transformed into the embodiment of a slick Sicilian club owner. My attire was meticulously chosen for this role: a sharp, tailored suit that spoke of wealth and taste, with a silk shirt open at the collar to suggest a hint of leisure and hedonism. A pair of polished leather shoes, gleaming under the studio's dim lights, completed the ensemble, their shine a testament to the meticulousness of my disguise. My hair was styled differently, slicked back to match the aesthetic of my assumed identity, and on my wrist, a watch gleamed with the suggestion of luxury—a necessary accessory for a man of my purported standing. This guise was meticulously crafted to engage Marco Velluti under terms he couldn't resist.

"Ah, Signor Ferro," Marco greeted me, his voice echoing slightly in the room crowded with computers, screens, mixers, and an array of musical instruments that spoke of his dedication—or perhaps obsession—

with his craft. He extended a hand heavy with rings, symbols of his success or perhaps just ostentation.

"So good of you to come. I've heard much of your prowess as a club owner," he continued, his eyes scrutinizing me, trying to pierce the facade I had so carefully constructed.

Taking his hand, I felt the cold metal of his rings against my skin, a stark contrast to the warmth of his welcome.

"Your reputation precedes you as well, Signor Velluti," I replied, allowing a hint of respect to color my tone. It was crucial that Marco saw me as a peer, an equal in this dance of deceit.

"Please, call me Marco," he insisted, a grandiose gesture encompassing the studio. Pride and arrogance intermingled on his face as he showcased his domain. "As you can see, I spare no expense in creating the finest soundscapes for my audience."

I nodded, my eyes sweeping over the equipment littering the space. Each piece was a testament to Marco's skill and relentless pursuit of sound perfection. But today, I was here to play a different tune—one that required Marco's expertise, not in the studio but at an event that would lack the presence of the unforgettable DJ Ecciti.

"Marco, I come with a proposal," I began, weaving my persona tighter around me like the final notes of a symphony. "Unfortunately, Ecciti won't be able to grace the party planned for the upcoming month at my club. We're seeking someone with your unique talents to fill the void, to captivate our audience as only you can."

The offer hung in the air between us, a tempting opportunity. Marco's interest was piqued, his earlier posture of casual arrogance shifting to one of keen attention. To be considered a replacement for Ecciti, even under these fabricated circumstances, was an honor that clearly appealed to him.

"Signor Ferro, you flatter me," Marco responded after a moment, the gleam in his eye betraying his interest. "To stand in for Ecciti is no small feat. Tell me more about this party. What vision do you have for it, and how do you see my music fitting into that tableau?"

As we delved into the details, the fictitious event taking shape in our conversation, I couldn't help but marvel at the ease with which lies can weave a reality of their own. Marco was now engaged, drawn into a narrative that, while false, served a greater truth in my quest to unravel the mystery surrounding Ecciti. My disguise as a Sicilian club owner had opened doors that Ferro, the private investigator, could never have nudged.

My gaze settled on a state-of-the-art computer, the screen displaying what appeared to be complex algorithms and waveforms. A thought wormed its way into my mind, and I sensed an opportunity to steer the conversation toward my true objective.

"You know, I've always been fascinated by the technical aspects of your craft. Just the other day, I was discussing DJ Ecciti's groundbreaking software with a colleague. Have you had a chance to explore it yourself?"

A flicker of... something crossed Marco's face before

his expression assumed a mask of indifference. "Ah, yes. I have heard of it, but I must confess I have not delved too deeply into its intricacies."

"Really?" I feigned surprise, watching him closely. "Given your penchant for cutting-edge technology, I would have thought it would be right up your alley. Rumor has it that another competitor's project bears a striking resemblance to DJ Ecciti's software. Surely you've heard the whispers?"

"Rumors are like smoke, Signore," Marco replied coolly, his fingers tapping a staccato rhythm on the console. "They drift and dissipate, leaving nothing but a trail of confusion."

"True," I conceded, my suspicions growing stronger. "But sometimes, where there is smoke, there is fire."

He glanced away, his evasiveness only fueling my desire to expose the truth. "Shall we discuss the collaboration you proposed?"

"Of course," I said, inwardly smirking at my small victory. But as we delved into the business at hand, I couldn't help but feel the irresistible pull of temptation, the allure of the hidden truths that lurked beneath Marco Velluti's carefully constructed facade.

"Speaking of engaging rhythms, Marco," I began, watching for any signs of distress in his eyes, "I've heard whispers that it could be possible that some people in the industry might have access to Ecciti's software. Do you think you can get it and use it at my party?"

The flicker of panic that darted across his face was as fleeting and electric as the touch of a lover's fingertips.

It sent a thrill through me, confirmed my suspicions, and I couldn't help but press harder.

Marco's response was swift, a dismissive wave of his hand cutting through the air like a conductor rebuffing an unsuitable note.

"That algorithm?" he scoffed, the notion seeming to offend him personally. "You misunderstand my art, Signor Ferro. My craft is born from the senses, from the tactile connection between man and machine, not from some cold, predefined set of instructions."

He paced the length of his small studio, gesturing passionately toward the array of instruments and equipment surrounding us.

"Music, true music, involves getting your hands dirty, diving into the depths of sound and emotion without a safety net. It's about discovery, exploration—not following a path laid out by someone else's calculations."

His intensity was palpable, a testament to his dedication to the traditional, hands-on approach to music production.

"Ecciti's algorithm might be a marvel to some, a shortcut to genius for others, but not for me," Marco declared, his voice resonating with a conviction that filled the room. As he spoke, he gestured towards a framed, purple, dried, and pressed flower hanging on the wall of his studio, an emblem of something personal and profound. "This," he said, his gaze lingering on the flower, "reminds me of the essence of gardening—nurturing, patience, and the human touch. My music," he continued, turning back with eyes ablaze with passion, "is like that garden. It's the product of intuition, of getting my hands dirty in the soil of sound and creativity. No software, no matter how advanced, can replicate the soulful connection between a creator and his creation."

The comparison struck a chord, painting a vivid picture of Marco's approach to his art—a dedication to craftsmanship that software, for all its precision, could never emulate.

As I left the studio, victory did not pulsate through my veins, but the feeling of uncertainty. Either Marco Velutti was genuinely against Ecciti's music algorithm, or he was putting up a very convincing facade. I knew I must continue to pursue the truth, no matter how dangerous or seductive it might prove to be.

*

The pulsing heart of San Marino had retreated to a whisper, the city's ancient stones exhaling their secrets as I navigated the shadowed alleys to meet Giancarlo Rossi. We convened in a secluded courtyard, where the shadows gave us receipt from the striking sun's heat. The scent of honeysuckle hung heavy in the air, its intoxicating fragrance mingling with the bitter tang of espresso wafting from a nearby café.

"Luigi Ferro," he greeted me, his dark eyes shimmering with gratitude and anguish in equal measure. "You've discovered something?"

"Maybe," I found myself saying, my voice threading through the uncertainty that clouded my thoughts. I relayed the encounter with Marco Velluti, the rival

DJ whose disdain for Ecciti's algorithm had revealed a complexity I hadn't anticipated. "But, he is surely envious of her success…"

"Ah, yes," Giancarlo exhaled, a mixture of relief and melancholy shading his response. "It's a tragedy, isn't it? How envy can suffocate brilliance."

"A tragedy indeed," I echoed, my gaze locked on him, searching for a hint of sincerity amidst the tumult of emotions. "Had you ever cautioned Aurelia about the perils her software might invite?"

"Si," he confessed, his anxiety manifesting in the way his fingers tangled with a silver chain at his neck. "I implored her to forsake the project, fearing it would usher in ruin and sorrow."

"And she resisted?" My question hung between us, laden with the weight of unspoken implications, as palpable as the current of a hidden stream.

"Stubborn, like all great artists," he murmured, a wistful smile tugging at the corners of his lips. "And perhaps… afraid that if she relented, she would lose herself."

In his words, I sensed a labyrinth of emotions and motives, a reflection of the intricate dance between ambition and caution. The conversation with Giancarlo had peeled back layers, revealing not just the risks associated with Ecciti's innovation but the profound complexities of human nature entwined with the pursuit of art and legacy.

"Was there anyone else who shared your concerns?" I inquired, my instincts honed to razor-sharp precision as I sensed the tantalizing hint of a deeper truth.

"Signorina Ricci," he confessed, his voice cracking with the weight of this revelation. "I asked her to step back from the project, too."

"Ricci?" I echoed, surprise mingling with suspicion as I considered this new piece of the puzzle. "You never mentioned her involvement before. How deep are her ties to this tangled web?"

"I don't really know," he admitted, his eyes clouded with uncertainty. "Perhaps she knew more than any of us. Perhaps… she was the key."

"Or perhaps," I mused, my thoughts a whirlwind of possibilities, "she is the lock that keeps the truth hidden away."

The air between us grew thick with tension, the silence as charged as the air before a storm. With each passing moment, the shadows seemed to close in, our shared quest for justice binding us as tightly as the embrace of star-crossed lovers.

"Stay vigilant, Giancarlo," I cautioned, my breath stirring the tendrils of honeysuckle that clung to the ancient walls like a lover's caress. "For we are navigating treacherous waters, and one false step could send us all plunging into the abyss."

"Si, Ferro," he replied, his gaze fixed on mine with an intensity that spoke of unspoken desires and secrets yet to be revealed.

With a final nod, I turned away and walked out of the courtyard. I traced a finger along the worn edge of an old brick wall, feeling the weight of centuries beneath my touch. The rival DJ, the software, and DJ Ecciti's death – it all swirled together in an intoxicating dance of deception and desire. But Giancarlo Rossi had provided the key, the final piece needed to unlock the door to the truth.

"No, this is about more than mere rivalry," I mused, my mind racing with a fierce urgency. "This is about power; the power to control, to dominate, to seduce."

My heart quickened at the realization. The theft of DJ Ecciti's software was not simply an act of jealousy; it was a calculated attempt to maintain the status quo to prevent her disruptive innovation from threatening the established order. And Signorina Ricci – sweet, beautiful Sofia – was deeply entangled in this deadly web.

My thoughts danced with images of Signorina Ricci, her sultry gaze promising secrets yet to be revealed. The soft curve of her lips, the delicate sweep of her neck – each detail a tantalizing hint of the passion that simmered beneath the surface.

"Time to set the trap," I whispered, determination steeling my resolve.

I knew I had to move quickly, for the serpent lay coiled in the shadows, ready to strike at any moment. With measured steps, I began to craft my plan: a lure to draw out the culprit and expose the extent of their involvement in the theft and murder.

By the time I reached Sofia Ricci's hotel, San Marino bathed in the orange glow of the setting sun. My heart pounded with anticipation, my mind whirling with desire and determination.

Her door opened to reveal Sofia in a luscious red dress, the color of freshly spilled blood. The sight of her took my breath away, and for a moment, I was a moth drawn to a flame.

"Luigi," she purred, her voice like velvet, wrapping around me and pulling me into her world. "I've been waiting for you."

"Sofia," I replied, stepping inside and closing the door behind me. "We have much to discuss."

She ordered room service, and over a dinner of osso buco and Barolo, our conversation flowed like the wine we sipped, rich and intoxicating. Each word from her lips was a symphony that stirred my soul while the light dancing in her eyes ignited a fire within me.

"Luigi," she asked, her voice tinged with urgency, "tell me what you've discovered."

"DJ Velluti is in some way implicated, maybe in both the software and Aureliai's death," I revealed, watching her reaction closely. "However, he's merely a pawn in a larger game."

"Who else is involved?" Her eyes narrowed, and a predatory gleam surfaced.

"Unknown, but it runs deep, Signorina," I confessed, feeling the weight of my duty press upon my chest. "We must tread carefully."

"Then we'll do it together," she vowed, laying her hand on mine. The touch sent electricity coursing through my veins, igniting a yearning that was difficult to suppress.

"Si, insieme," I agreed, my voice a hoarse whisper. "But we must not let our desire derail us."

"Of course," she replied with a knowing smile that

promised untold delights. "But tonight, let us indulge in the passion that threatens to consume us."

"Only if you promise me one thing," I said, my heart thundering in my chest as I leaned closer, our lips mere inches apart.

"Anything," she breathed, her eyes heavy with longing.

"Once this is over, you'll help me set up a trap to get justice for DJ Ecciti and bring those responsible to their knees."

"Agreed," she whispered and sealed our pact with a searing kiss that set my world ablaze.

As our bodies entwined in the dimly lit suite, the line between justice and desire blurred into oblivion, and San Marino's ancient heartbeat thrummed in time with our own. And in that moment of shared passion, we vowed to conquer the darkness that dared to threaten our city and those we held dear.

7

The scent of freshly brewed coffee mingled with Sofia Ricci's intoxicating perfume as she lay elegantly sprawled across the silken sheets. I could not resist a sidelong glance at her disheveled beauty before focusing my attention on the steaming cappuccino and delicate pastries that adorned the breakfast tray. As I sipped the coffee, its bitterness was a welcome contrast to the sweetness of the morning, and I felt an urgent need to discuss the matter at hand.

"Honey," I began, my voice as smooth as the silk beneath us, "we must talk about tonight's little show. It is crucial that you understand your part in this intricate dance."

Sofia shifted in the bed, her dark curls cascading over her bare shoulders as she met my gaze, her eyes full of questions and curiosity. "Ferro, tell me what I must do to ensure the success of our plan." Her voice was a sultry murmur, the very essence of temptation.

"Listen carefully, Sofia," I began, my voice low and measured. "We must ensnare these bidders, and you'll play a crucial role." She raised an eyebrow, a hint of mischief playing at the corners of her mouth. "You're going to act as both yourself and a bidder for the software."

She leaned closer, the heat from her body seeping into mine. "I do love a dangerous game, Ferro," she whispered seductively. "Tell me more."

"First, you must play yourself – the beautiful and enigmatic Sofia Ricci. You know how to use your charm and allure to captivate those around you," I said, gesturing towards her inviting figure with a mixture of admiration and desire. "But when it comes to the bidding, your job is to drive up the price, making the others fight harder for it. Anything to make them more desperate and reckless. We need them off balance, vulnerable to making mistakes." I paused, watching as she considered the plan, the gears turning behind her emerald eyes. "Do you think you can handle that?"

"Darling, I've been playing men like these my entire life," she replied with a wicked grin. "Consider it done."

"Excellent," I said, finishing the last of my coffee. A plan began to take shape in my mind, a web of deception that would ensnare our enemies and leave them powerless. "Now, there's one more thing we need to do before the trap is set."

"Which is?" Sofia asked, her eyes intent on mine.

"Spread false information about the recovered software," I said, my voice laced with anticipation. "We need to make sure every greedy bastard in the music and tech industries hears about it. They won't be able to resist such a tempting prize."

"Sounds like fun," she purred, her fingers tracing patterns on the sheets. "I'll make a few calls and see what strings I can pull."

"Good," I replied, my heart pounding with excitement as the pieces fell into place. This game of desire, temptation, and power was intoxicating, and I couldn't wait to see it unfold.

As I left her bedroom, my thoughts were consumed by the trap we were setting and the knowledge that soon, our enemies would be dancing to our tune. The rhythm of deceit and seduction pulsed through me, sending shivers down my spine. It was time for the show to begin.

*

The sun dipped low in the sky, casting long shadows over the cobblestone streets as I made my way back to Sofia's hotel. The air was thick with the musky scent of autumn leaves mingling with the fumes of espresso and the irresistible fragrance of fresh-baked bread. I couldn't help but feel invigorated by the atmosphere, my heart racing like the Vespas zipping past me.

"Ferro," a smooth voice purred from behind me. Sofia emerged from the hotel entrance, her figure-hugging black dress leaving little to the imagination. "Everything is arranged for our little soiree."

"Perfect," I replied, my gaze lingering on her momentarily before turning toward the grand hotel. No expense had been spared in its design, the marble facade depicting scenes from ancient Rome, hinting at the power and opulence hidden within.

The conference room we had chosen for our trap lay deep within the hotel's inner sanctum, shielded from prying eyes by layers of discretion and wealth. As I approached the room, I felt a thrill of anticipation run down my spine, knowing that soon, our enemies would be playing into our hands.

"Welcome, lady and gentlemen," I said, my voice

resonating through the dimly lit room as the bidders took their seats. I was careful not to reveal too much, a master of hiding my true intentions. "My name is Luigi Ferro, and tonight, I present you with an opportunity of a lifetime."

"Opportunity?" one bidder raised an eyebrow, skepticism etched across his face.

"Indeed," I responded, pausing to let the word hang heavy in the air. "For today, we offer you exclusive access to groundbreaking software that has recently come into my possession. Recovered from the ashes of a terrible crime, this software has the potential to revolutionize the way we create and consume music."

"Ah," another bidder interjected, his fingers drumming on the table, "and I suppose you expect us to simply take your word for it?"

"Of course not," I smirked, my tone laced with amusement. "Each of you will have the chance to verify its authenticity before bidding commences. But let me assure you – once you've seen what this software can do, you won't be able to resist the temptation."

Their eyes flickered with greed, curiosity, and even hunger as they considered my words. These men knew the price of power, and I could see in their expressions that they were more than willing to pay it.

"Very well," one of them conceded, his voice dripping with barely contained desire. "Show us what you have, Mr. Ferro. Let us see if your prize is truly worth our time."

"Patience, gentlemen," I said with a sly smile, knowing that the seeds of temptation had been sown.

"All will be revealed in due time. For now, I must ask you to enjoy the refreshments provided and prepare yourselves for the bidding war to come."

As they milled about the room, I caught Sofia's eye from across the space. She gave me a subtle nod, her gaze smoldering with the knowledge of our shared secret. The trap was set, and soon, our enemies would find themselves entangled in a web of desire and deception.

The door to the conference room swung open, revealing a tableau of intrigue as Luca Bianchi, Marco Velutti, and Giancarlo Rossi entered the lair of our twisted game. The air hung heavy with suspicion, each man eyeing the other as if they could unravel their intentions with a mere glance. I watched them from my vantage point, observing their movements, taking in every nuance of their body language, seeking any hint that might betray their true nature.

"Ah, gentlemen," I greeted, raising my glass of Barolo in salute. "Welcome to this exclusive gathering. I trust you've found your way here without too much difficulty?"

"Cut the pleasantries, Ferro," snapped Giancarlo, his eyes narrowed in impatience. "We're not here for wine and idle chit-chat."

"Of course not," I agreed smoothly, setting my glass down and folding my hands behind my back. "You're here for something far more... enticing."

I felt Sofia's gaze on me like a caress, her presence in the room adding another layer of seduction to the proceedings. She knew how to play her part well, and I had no doubt she would use her charms to manipulate the situation to our advantage.

"Indeed," murmured a software developer from Rome, his voice tinged with curiosity. Your invitation was quite suggestive, Signor Ferro. You claim to possess a groundbreaking piece of software—one that could revolutionize the music industry, no less."

"An exaggeration, perhaps?" ventured Marco Velutti, his fingers tapping rhythmically on the table, betraying his eagerness.

"Ah, gentlemen, I assure you, there is nothing exaggerated about the power this software holds." My words dripped with temptation, drawing them further into the web we'd spun. "But, as I mentioned in my invitation, this opportunity is not for the faint of heart. Are you prepared to engage in a little... friendly competition?"

"Your terms were clear," interjected Luca Bianchi, a man of few words but with a reputation for ruthless ambition. "We're here to play, Ferro. But know that we don't take kindly to being played ourselves."

"Neither do I, Signor Bianchi," I replied, my tone deceptively mild. "Which is why you can trust that this game will be both fair and rewarding – for the victor."

The tension in the room tightened like a noose, each man sizing up his opponents with barely concealed hatred. Their eyes darted from one to another, seeking any sign of weakness they could exploit.

"Then let us proceed," said Giancarlo, his voice thick with anticipation. "Show us what you have, Ferro, and let the real games begin."

I surveyed the room, my gaze lingering on the predatory gleams in the bidders' eyes: Luca Bianchi, his tailored suit a testament to his wealth; Marco Velutti, a calculating smile playing on his lips; the software developer from Rome, his fingers twitching with barely restrained eagerness; and Giancarlo, whose piercing stare seemed to bore through my very soul.

"Then let's begin," I announced, my voice resonating with authority. "As you are well aware, we have gathered here today for a unique opportunity – one that promises untold fortunes for the fortunate few who possess the audacity to seize it."

"Enough with the theatrics, Ferro," interrupted Marco, his impatience palpable. "We know why we're here. Get to the point."

"Of course," I assented, allowing a hint of amusement to color my tone. "Lady and gentlemen, the auction will proceed as follows: each bid must be made in increments of no less than €50,000. Cash or certified bank checks only. The highest bidder wins possession of the software. If at any time someone makes a bid that no one else is willing to surpass, they will be declared the winner."

"Sounds simple enough," muttered the software developer, his gaze never leaving the black velvet case stationed prominently on the table before us.

"Indeed," I agreed, my eyes flickering to Sofia, who sat on the first row of chairs with crossed legs that exposed more than most men could resist. "But let me assure you, gentlemen, that every precaution has been taken to ensure this auction is conducted fairly and discreetly. No outside interference will be tolerated, and any attempt at ill faith will be met with swift and severe consequences. Are we clear?"

"Crystal," replied Giancarlo, his voice dripping with disdain.

"Very well," I said, a sly grin tugging at the corners of my mouth. "Let the bidding commence."

"€500,000," declared Luca, his voice brimming with confidence.

"€550,000," countered Marco, his eyes narrowing as they locked onto Luca's.

"€600,000," chimed in the software developer, the first signs of sweat beading on his brow.

"€700,000," Giancarlo proclaimed, his tone arrogant, as if daring anyone to outbid him.

"One million," Sofia interjected, her voice smooth as velvet, seductive as sin.

As the bids escalated, so too did the tension in the room, each man fueled by an insatiable thirst for power and control. My fingers drummed rhythmically against the table, a silent conductor orchestrating a symphony of desire and deception while contemplating the melody yet to be played.

The air in the room, heavy with anticipation, clung to my skin like silk against the curves of a lover. My eyes danced from bidder to bidder, my breath hitching ever so slightly as the bidding intensified.

"€1,200,000," Sofia purred, her gaze settling on Giancarlo, who met her stare with a mix of desire and frustration.

"€1,400,000," countered Luca, beads of sweat now trickling down his temples.

"€1,500,000," offered the software developer, desperation etched into his every feature.

"€2,000,000," came Sofia's sultry voice, her eyes alight with the flames of temptation.

"Enough!" Giancarlo barked, the word echoing through the chamber like the peal of a funeral bell. "Damn you," snarled Giancarlo, his face contorted with rage.

Silence enveloped the room like a velvet shroud; no one dared draw breath lest they disturb the delicate balance of power that hung in the air.

"Two million. Going once," I intoned, my voice resonating through the hushed chamber as I walked up to Sofia, handing her the USB stick."Going twice... Sold."

The air in the room, thick with tension and avarice, suddenly shifted as a man erupted into motion, his trajectory aimed squarely at Sofia. The collective gasp of surprise echoed like a gunshot in the dimly lit chamber.

"Sofia!" I shouted, my voice barely audible above the din of confusion that ensued.

The man struck her down with a swift blow, the force of his attack sending her tumbling to the ground. The USB stick tumbled from her delicate fingers, skittering across the floor like a frightened insect in search of sanctuary.

"Get down!" someone bellowed, throwing himself on the floor for protection.

I lunged forward, but my fingers closed on empty air as the attacker slipped away, vanishing into the shadows like a ghost. The room swam before my eyes, a vortex of color and sound that seemed to blur together, the edges fraying like the threads of a worn tapestry.

"Damn you!" I spat, the words a curse that clung to the air between us, heavy with the weight of a thousand unspoken promises.

As the room descended further into chaos, I knelt beside Sofia's unconscious form, my hand trembling as I pressed it against her still-warm skin. Her breaths were shallow, each a fragile whisper that threatened to fade into silence, leaving only the echoes of memory behind.

"Stay with me, Sofia," I pleaded, my heart breaking beneath the burden of guilt and despair that threatened to crush me. "Don't leave me now."

8

The gendarmerie loomed before me, its gray facade casting a long shadow on the street as I parked my Vespa.

"Ah, Ferro!" Capparoni greeted me as I pushed open the door. His booming voice cut through the tense atmosphere like a finely honed blade. "Glad you could make it. Our boys managed to apprehend the attacker at the hotel's exit."

"Velutti?" I inquired, my brow furrowing with curiosity and anticipation.

"Indeed," he affirmed, his eyes narrowing in gravity. "Come, he's waiting for us in the interrogation room."

The air inside the gendarmerie was thick with tension—officers scurrying about in a frenzied dance, their whispers a cacophony of speculation and unease. It was clear that the high-profile case had struck a chord among them, the weight of responsibility laid bare for all to see.

Capparoni led me down a narrow hallway, our footsteps muffled by the worn carpet beneath us. He stopped before a nondescript door, the brass handle gleaming in the dim light. As he opened it, a waft of stale air assaulted my senses, a subtle yet unmistakable reminder of the countless confessions extracted within these walls.

"Buona fortuna, Ferro," Capparoni murmured, his

voice low and sad. He retreated, leaving me alone with my quarry.

There he was—Marco Velutti, seated in the center of the small, windowless room. His eyes, a stormy mix of defiance and fear, met mine with an intensity that sent a shiver down my spine. The scent of stale sweat and desperation hung heavy in the air, mingling with the lingering traces of expensive cologne.

"So, Marco," I began, my voice smooth as silk. "How the mighty have fallen."

"Save your platitudes, Ferro," he spat, his voice a venomous hiss. "I know why I'm here."

"Of course," I mused, circling him like a predator stalking its prey. "You stand accused of a most heinous crime—the murder of DJ Ecciti. Tell me, what could drive a man such as yourself to commit such a vile act?"

"Your words are wasted on me, detective," he sneered, his fear momentarily overshadowed by contempt. "I've nothing to say to the likes of you."

"Perhaps," I conceded, allowing a hint of a smile to play at the corners of my lips. "But I have a feeling that won't last for long."

The room seemed to close in around us, the walls whispering their sordid secrets as we locked ourselves in a battle of wits and wills. But I would not be deterred. Justice would be served, and the truth would come to light. In this dance of desire and temptation, power and seduction, secrecy and deception—I would emerge triumphant.

"Let's talk about the software, shall we?" I ventured, my voice a velvety caress that slid beneath Velutti's defenses. "DJ Ecciti's algorithm can revolutionize the DJ world, disrupting the status quo you hold so dear. That must have been quite… unsettling for you."

Velutti shifted in his seat, the telltale flicker of unease dancing across his face like shadows cast by candlelight.

"What are you implying, Ferro?"

"Nothing more than what the evidence suggests," I replied, savoring the taste of each word as it rolled off my tongue. "You had motive, means, and opportunity. A deadly cocktail, wouldn't you say?"

"You have no proof. Your accusations are baseless," he retorted, a thin veneer of bravado masking the tremor in his voice.

"Are they now?" I mused, allowing my gaze to wander the room, drinking in every detail with an insatiable hunger. My eyes came to rest on a framed picture hanging on the wall behind him—a dried flower nestled within its depths. The foxglove, a symbol of temptation and deceit, was also the very poison used to snuff out DJ Ecciti's life.

"It seems fate has a sense of humor," I whispered, the words dripping with honeyed venom. "The very instrument of your crime adorning your studio's wall. How fitting."

His eyes widened, pupils dilated with a heady cocktail of fear and disbelief. He tried to mask it, but the truth was etched into every crease and contour of his face. Velutti was unraveling, and I reveled in the intoxicating power of his undoing.

"Enough!" He shouted, his voice echoing through

the small room like the peal of a church bell. "I don't know what you're talking about!"

"Ah, but I think you do," I responded, my words a silken caress that wound their way around his throat, tightening their grip with every syllable. "And soon enough, so will the world."

I could feel the electric thrill of victory coursing through my veins like the finest vintage. In this game of seduction and deception, where secrets were currency and lies the very fabric of our existence, the truth would always emerge victorious.

And as I stood there, bathed in the dying embers of Velutti's defiance, I knew that justice would be served—and the rhythm of murder would beat its final, resounding note.

The air in the room grew thick, suffocating, as if some ancient curse had been unleashed upon us. Velutti's composure crumbled before my very eyes, his once-imperious façade dissolving like sugar in the espresso of truth. Sweat bloomed on his brow, a glistening field that betrayed the tempest raging within him. His hands trembled, each quiver an involuntary admission of guilt.

"Alright, Ferro," he spat, his voice choked with the bitter bile of defeat. I did it. I poisoned that hack of a DJ. What choice did I have? Her software threatened everything we'd built, every last morsel of power and prestige that was the core of our industry."

"Power and prestige, Marco, are not earned through deception and murder," I replied, my tone measured and cold as steel. "You've gambled with the fates and lost."

Velutti glared at me, his eyes smoldering embers of hate and humiliation. But there was no fire left to fuel his rage, only the ashes of a man who'd succumbed to his darkest desires.

*

Leaving the gendarmerie, I straddled my faithful Vespa, its engine purring like a contented feline beneath me. As I navigated the labyrinthine streets of San Marino, the balmy caress of the wind whispered sweet victory in my ear. Yet, as I neared the hospital where Sofia lay, a gnawing worry began to nibble at the edges of my triumph.

The sterile halls of the hospital echoed with hushed secrets as I entered Sofia's dimly lit room, my heart pounding a staccato rhythm against my ribs. Slivers of moonlight streamed through the window, casting her pale form in an ethereal glow.

"Sofia," I whispered, my voice barely audible above the hum of the air conditioner. "I have brought justice to our fallen DJ. You are safe now."

"Safe?" she replied, her eyes clouded with pain and exhaustion, as if those simple words weighed heavy upon her soul. "From the darkness that festers within us all?"

"Perhaps not," I conceded, my thoughts swirling like autumn leaves caught in a whirlwind of uncertainty. "But for now, at least, we can breathe a little easier."

Standing beside her bed, I considered the tangled

web we'd woven and the dark temptations that had trapped us all. The rhythm of murder, it seemed, had been silenced for now—but would it ever truly fade away?

Only time would tell.

The midday sun draped itself around Sofia's fragile form, a siren of gold and shadows. The air was thick with the scent of antiseptic, and the steady beep of machines punctuated the silence as if to remind us that life and death danced cheek to cheek in this cold, sterile chamber. A shiver slithered down my spine, but whether it was from the chill of the room or the weight of what we had uncovered, I could not say.

"Ah, Sofia," I murmured, my soul trembling like a sparrow caught in a storm, "Justice has found its mark, and Velutti will pay for his crimes."

"Is it truly over?" she whispered, her voice as delicate as the threads of a spider's web. Her eyes, dark mirrors reflecting the secrets of the night, met mine with a flicker of gratitude piercing through the exhaustion that clung to her like a funeral shroud.

"Si, cara mia," I replied, allowing a ghost of a smile to touch my lips. "The darkness has been chased away, at least for now." Relief washed over her features as if a gentle tide had swept away the anguish that had haunted her since fate had cast us together in this twisted dance of desire and deceit.

"DJ Ecciti's memory weighs heavy on me, Luigi," Sofia confessed, her fingers tracing invisible patterns on the starched hospital sheets. "I cannot let her legacy vanish into the shadows."

"Her music will live on," I assured her, my heart swelling with pride at her resilience. "And you, Sofia, will be the one to carry it forward."

Her eyes widened, surprise mingling with determination. "Yes, Luigi. I will ensure that her groundbreaking software finds a home in an open-source community so that her artistry continues to thrive."

"Brava, Sofia," I praised, my voice a velvet caress as the shadows deepened around us. "You honor her memory and prove that temptation and power need not always be wielded for evil."

"Even in darkness, there is light," she whispered, her gaze never leaving mine, as if she sought to share some secret truth known only to those who had danced with desire and emerged unscathed.

"Si," I replied, sitting down on the bed next to her bruised body. "There is always light, as long as we dare to seek it."

The air in the hospital room hung heavy with the weight of our unspoken words, a tangible testament to the passion and pain that had brought us to this precipice. Even in her weakened state, Sofia, ever the icon of strength and beauty, held my gaze with unwavering determination as I vowed to support her in honoring DJ Ecciti's legacy.

"Your decision is admirable, Sofia," I murmured, my voice barely more than a silken whisper. "You have my word; I will be by your side throughout this journey."

"Thank you, Luigi," she replied, her eyes alight with gratitude and the fire of a thousand suns. "Together, we will ensure that Aurelia's vision lives on, untainted by the darkness that sought to consume it."

We shared a moment of quiet reflection, the silence punctuated only by the distant murmur of voices and the rhythmic beating of our hearts. It was in these stolen moments that the full weight of the case settled upon my shoulders, a heavy burden tempered only by the knowledge that justice had been served.

"Death, like desire, has its own rhythm," I mused aloud, my thoughts wandering to the intricate dance between predator and prey that had played out before us. "It is a force that can seduce even the most virtuous of souls, drawing them into its dark embrace."

"The rhythm of death," Sofia agreed, her voice laced with sorrow and understanding. "But it is also a reminder of the fleeting nature of life and the importance of living each moment to its fullest."

"Rest now, Sofia," I urged her gently, knowing that the trials of the day had taken their toll on her body and spirit. "Tomorrow is a new beginning."

"Thank you," she whispered, her eyes closing in exhaustion as the tendrils of sleep began to weave their spell around her. "Grazie mille, mio eroe."

The amber glow of the bar lights reflected in my gin, swirling with a twist of lime. I savored the sharp tang as it slithered down my throat, igniting a fire within me that mirrored the far-reaching consequences of the case I had just closed. The music and tech industries would never be the same; the murder of DJ Ecciti had sent tremors through their very foundations, sparking heated discussions about innovation, ownership, and legacy.

As I sat there, surrounded by the seductive murmur of conversations and the clink of glasses, I couldn't help but contemplate the nature of justice in a digital age. The world had grown ever more entwined in the tendrils of technology, but what did it mean for the delicate balance of morality? The city's ancient walls, steeped in history, seemed to mock our feeble attempts at grappling with the implications of this new world order.

"Perché così pensieroso?" The bartender, a wiry man with eyes that held depths one could drown in, questioned me.

"Justice, mio amico. It's a fickle thing," I replied, sipping my gin.

"Ah, la giustizia," he mused, polishing a glass with slow, deliberate motions. "It has been sought since the dawn of time, yet it remains elusive."

"Indeed," I murmured, my thoughts wandering back

to the complexities of the case. The threads of desire, temptation, and power that had woven a deadly web around the players involved still haunted me. How many other lives had been ensnared, caught in the crossfire of ambition and greed?

I relished the cool touch of the glass against my skin, the condensation weaving a trail down its side like a tear. The very fabric of our society was being tested, stretched thin by the weight of humanity's insatiable hunger for knowledge and mastery. In the face of such monumental change, could our age-old concepts of justice still hold true?

"Sometimes, I wonder whether we've lost sight of what really matters," I admitted, my voice barely more than a whisper, lest the shadows of the past emerge to challenge my words.

"Perhaps, but we must continue to strive for what is right, no matter the cost," the bartender counseled, his eyes locked on mine with steely determination. "For if we lose ourselves along the way, what hope do we have?"

Before I could respond, the shrill ring of my phone cut through the air like a knife. It was Di Mauro asking me to come down to SMTV for one last meeting. I knew that this was the moment where the remaining strands of this intricate web would be drawn together, the final truths revealed and exposed to the light.

I nodded a silent thank you to the bartender as I left. The sun dipped low on the horizon, casting a golden glow upon the festival grounds as I gazed out from the bar's window. The air was thick with anticipation and nostalgia as the final chords of music reverberated through the twilight expanse. Like an ancient ritual, the closing ceremony of the festival unfolded before me—a bittersweet symphony of lights and shadows that marked both the end of one era and the dawning of another.

As I stepped out into the cool night air, I made my way towards the SMTV offices, my thoughts preoccupied with the case that had consumed me these past days. The air was crisp, a refreshing change from the stifling tension of uncovering truths hidden in the shadows of the music industry. It was on this reflective journey that I unexpectedly bumped into Giancarlo Rossi as he was departing the Grand Hotel, his bags in hand, signaling a departure that seemed laden with more than just physical weight.

"Ah, Ferro," Giancarlo greeted me, a trace of surprise in his voice quickly overshadowed by a weary resignation. "I was just leaving town. I heard about what happened with Velutti."

We fell into step, the rhythm of our conversation mirroring our strides. I shared with him the outcome of the convoluted events that had trapped us all, detailing how Velutti would face justice for his crimes and, most importantly, how Aurelia's groundbreaking algorithm would soon be released into the public domain, a tribute to her genius and a gift to the music world she had left behind.

Giancarlo's response was a mixture of relief and melancholy. "That's good to hear, Ferro. It's what Aurelia would have wanted," he said, a sense of closure softening the lines of his face. "Her legacy will live on, not just in our memories but in the music that will continue to be created because of her work."

We parted ways at the edge of the square, Giancarlo heading towards a future untethered from the tragedy that had overshadowed his recent days. At the same time, I continued on to SMTV, the final act of this intricate play yet to unfold.

Approaching the SMTV offices, I encountered Luca Bianchi, the manager whose initial annoyance at my intrusion was palpable. "Ferro," he began, his tone sharp, "that auction stunt you pulled… It was reckless. You could have ruined everything."

His words hung between us, a reminder of the fine line I had walked in orchestrating the deception that had ensnared Velutti and exposed the underbelly of their world. I waited, allowing him the space to air his grievances, knowing that the resolution of the case had brought about a complex mix of outcomes.

But as Bianchi continued, his tone shifted, the edges of his frustration softening with a begrudging respect. "Despite it all, I can't deny the outcome," he conceded, a hint of a smile breaking through his earlier facade of annoyance. "Velutti's gone, yes, and we've lost two great DJs to the dance market. But Aurelia's algorithm is being made public. It's a game-changer. It could revolutionize how we create music."

The acknowledgment of the bigger picture, of the impact Aurelia's work would have on the industry, seemed to bring Luca a sense of perspective. It was a bittersweet victory, marred by loss but underscored by the potential for innovation and growth.

*

The pungent aroma of espresso, mingling with the lingering scent of a woman's perfume, greeted me as I entered the SMTV building. The once bustling halls now felt subdued, the tangible tension dissolving in the wake of DJ Ecciti's murder resolution.

"Signor Ferro!" A voice called out, and I turned to see the receptionist, her face flushed with gratitude. "Thank you," she whispered, her eyes shimmering with unshed tears. "You've brought justice for Ecciti and restored her legacy."

As I continued down the corridor, lost in my thoughts, I almost collided with Di Mauro, who stood waiting near his office door. He extended his hand, a gesture tempered by solemnity and respect.

"Luigi, we owe you our deepest gratitude for untangling this twisted web," he said, his words a balm to the wounds inflicted by this case. "Your investigation has not only brought closure to those affected, but it has also shown how essential your skills are in navigating the treacherous waters of our industry."

"Your praise is humbling, Di Mauro," I admitted, clasping his hand firmly. "However, the pursuit of truth and justice drives me, not accolades."

"Si, I know," he said, nodding gravely. "And yet, your work has made an indelible mark on the fabric of our society, reminding us all of the power of truth to heal and restore."

"Thank you, Di Mauro," I replied, feeling the weight of my role in this tale of seduction and secrecy.

As I left SMTV behind, the cool night air embraced me, whispering secrets of its own. I knew that despite the closure we had found, the threads of temptation and desire would continue to weave their way through our lives – an eternal dance between darkness and light. And as a guardian of truth, I would always stand ready, my senses honed and my heart steadfast, prepared to unravel the mysteries that lay hidden beneath the gossamer veils of life's many passions.

Despite my victory, my steps were heavy up the street to my flat. Two artists who had given so much joy to their fans were gone. But as I continued my slow stroll, I couldn't help but marvel at the resilience of this city – its inhabitants weaving a tapestry of hope and renewal from the threads of tragedy. The air hummed with quiet determination as if each breath carried with it a whispered promise: We will overcome. We will endure.

I took solace in that thought, drawing strength from the knowledge that even in our darkest hour, there remained a flicker of light – a beacon guiding us through the tempest and into the calm embrace of redemption.

And so, as the night set on San Marino and the darkness enveloped it, I felt a weight lift from my shoulders – a burden borne by the collective heart of this ancient city, now released into the gathering night. And in that moment, I knew that whatever challenges lay ahead, we would face them together, united by truth and bound by the indomitable spirit of our shared humanity.

The End

"Signor Ferro," a timid voice called through the door, "I... I have your payment."

The door creaked open, revealing a young man with a red face and trembling hands. He held out an envelope stuffed with cash, the weight of the bills heavy with both relief and regret.As we walked toward her abode, I allowed myself a moment to savor the taste of her, the intoxicating blend of wine and desire that lingered on my tongue. It was a potent reminder of the life that awaited me beyond the shadows – a world filled with pleasure and temptation, where the seductive lure of secrecy blurred the lines between love and power.

THE END

LUIGI FERRO
WILL RETURN

A Story from

Yesteryear's Stories Reflected Today
Yabot AB
www.yabot.se

9 789189 822665